Amy Cross is the author of more than 100 horror, paranormal, fantasy and thriller novels.

OTHER TITLES
BY AMY CROSS INCLUDE

*American Coven*
*Annie's Room*
*The Ash House*
*Asylum*
*B&B*
*The Bride of Ashbyrn House*
*The Camera Man*
*The Curse of Wetherley House*
*The Devil, the Witch and the Whore*
*Devil's Briar*
*The Dog*
*Eli's Town*
*The Farm*
*The Ghost of Molly Holt*
*The Ghosts of Lakeforth Hotel*
*The Girl Who Never Came Back*
*Haunted*
*The Haunting of Blackwych Grange*
*Like Stones on a Crow's Back*
*The Night Girl*
*Perfect Little Monsters & Other Stories*
*Stephen*
*The Shades*
*The Soul Auction*
*Tenderling*
*Ward Z*

# THE HAUNTING OF THE CROWFORD HOY

AMY CROSS

This edition
first published by Blackwych Books Ltd
United Kingdom, 2021

Copyright © 2021 Amy Cross

All rights reserved. This book is a work of fiction. Names, characters, places, incidents and businesses are the product of the author's imagination or are used fictitiously. Any resemblance to actual persons, living or dead, or to actual events or locations, is entirely coincidental.

Also available in e-book format.

www.blackwychbooks.com

# CONTENTS

PROLOGUE
*page 15*

CHAPTER ONE
*page 23*

CHAPTER TWO
*page 31*

CHAPTER THREE
*page 39*

CHAPTER FOUR
*page 47*

CHAPTER FIVE
*page 55*

CHAPTER SIX
*page 63*

CHAPTER SEVEN
*page 71*

CHAPTER EIGHT
*page 79*

CHAPTER NINE
*page 87*

CHAPTER TEN
*page 95*

CHAPTER ELEVEN
*page 103*

CHAPTER TWELVE
*page 111*

CHAPTER THIRTEEN
*page 119*

CHAPTER FOURTEEN
*page 127*

CHAPTER FIFTEEN
*page 135*

CHAPTER SIXTEEN
*page 143*

CHAPTER SEVENTEEN
*page 151*

CHAPTER EIGHTEEN
*page 159*

CHAPTER NINETEEN
*page 167*

CHAPTER TWENTY
*page 175*

CHAPTER TWENTY-ONE
*page 183*

CHAPTER TWENTY-TWO
*page 191*

CHAPTER TWENTY-THREE
*page 199*

CHAPTER TWENTY-FOUR
*page 207*

CHAPTER TWENTY-FIVE
*page 215*

CHAPTER TWENTY-SIX
*page 223*

CHAPTER TWENTY-SEVEN
*page 231*

CHAPTER TWENTY-EIGHT
*page 239*

CHAPTER TWENTY-NINE
*page 247*

CHAPTER THIRTY
*page 255*

EPILOGUE
*page 263*

# THE HAUNTING OF THE CROWFORD HOY

# PROLOGUE

*January 5$^{th}$, 1984...*

"JERRY, GET ANOTHER ROUND in for everyone!"

A roar immediately filled the room. Packed around the bar area, the Crowford Hoy regulars began to quickly finish their drinks, as Jerry grabbed a couple of glasses and started pouring more pints.

"Hell must've frozen over," Percy suggested, as he wiped some stray beer from his chin, "if Gary Newcroft's buying us all a drink."

"Share and share alike," Gary replied, leafing through a wad of notes. "I said I'd stand everyone a drink if that horse came in, and I'm not gonna weasel out now."

"Didn't you say you'd buy us all a bottle of champagne?" Stevie Mercer suggested.

"I don't remember that at all," Gary said as laughter rang out. "No, I definitely didn't say anything about champagne."

As everyone shouted their orders to Jerry, not one person noticed that somebody was trying to get the front door open. Rain was lashing down outside, and for a moment the figure in the hooded raincoat struggled to get through. Once she was inside, however, she pulled her hood back and stood dripping on the mat, watching the furore at the bar. Out of breath and exhausted, she began to make her way across the room, although the crowd of people meant that she wasn't entirely sure which route to take.

"Excuse me," she said, trying to dodge between two of the men. "I'm sorry, I..."

Her voice trailed off as she realized that they still hadn't noticed her. She glanced over her shoulder, looking at the window and seeing the lights of her car in the darkness, and then she turned back toward the bar. She knew she didn't have long, so finally she turned and hurried around past the fireplace, taking the long route all the way through the far seating area before stepping over some stools and finally managing to squeeze over to the service hatch.

"I'll be with you in a second, love," Jerry told her.

"Actually, I'm just -"

Before she could finish, Jerry headed over to the other side of the bar.

"You'll have to forgive him," Malcolm said, turning to the woman, "he's bloody useless. It's not his fault, though. He's only had eight years to get it right."

She tried to smile, but she was too panicked, too worried about each precious second that was ticking past. She looked toward the window again, and then she saw that the landlord – Jerry Butler was his name, she knew that much from their phone conversations – was still frantically trying to pour as many pints as possible. She wanted to call out to him, but all the voices around her were so loud, she knew he'd most likely never hear. Besides, the last thing she wanted to do was seem pushy. She knew she couldn't afford to make a bad impression.

"Jerry!" George yelled, before pointing at the woman. "Where are your manners, son? There's a lady waiting for a drink!"

"I know there's a lady waiting for a drink," Jerry muttered, bending down to take two more glasses from one of the shelves. He glanced at the woman. "I'll be two seconds, love, I promise."

"He's a charmer, isn't he?" George said with a smile as he looked at the woman.

"I just..."

Again, her voice trailed off. In all the madness of the room, she knew there was no way she could attract Jerry's attention, but she also knew that she couldn't take much longer. She was frantically trying to think of a way to get him to notice her, when he suddenly broke off from talking to two men and made his way over.

"Hang on, lads!" he called out. "I'm serving the lady and then I'll be back to you." He stopped in front of the woman. "Sorry about that. What can I get you?"

"The key," she replied. "Please..."

"I beg your pardon?"

She wiped some wet, matted hair from across the face.

"My name's Sally Cooper," she told him. "We spoke on the phone, I'm your new barmaid. Uh, live-in barmaid. I'm going to be working here."

"I'm so sorry," he replied with a sigh, "I completely forgot you were coming tonight. You must think I'm completely disorganized." He turned and waved at the others. "Lads, this is Sally! She's the new barmaid I told you about, she's moved here all the way from..."

He glanced back at her.

"Where did you say you were moving here from, again?"

"London," she replied, feeling a little uncomfortable as she realized that everyone was now looking at her. "The thing is, my car's outside and I was thinking I should get my things in. You said there's a side door..."

"There is," he replied, reaching behind the counter and grabbing a set of keys, which he then handed to her. "It's best to use that door if you want to avoid this rowdy lot, it'll take you right through into the hall and then you can get upstairs. But listen, why don't you grab a drink and meet some of the regulars, and then I'll help you up with your things after?"

"Thanks, but I'd really rather do it now," she told him.

"Then I'll get one of these useless ingrates to help you," he replied, turning to look along the bar. "Fellas, who wants to -"

"No!" Sally blurted out before he could finish. "Really, that's very kind of you, but I'd rather do it myself. Thank you again. I'll be down shortly."

Without waiting for anyone to try to stop

her, she headed back out the way she'd come, politely acknowledging all the people who tried to introduce themselves but making sure to not get held up. She'd already taken far too long to fetch the key, even if she also worried that she might have seemed a little rude. By the time she got to the door, she realized she'd probably made a really bad impression, but when she looked back toward the bar she realized that everyone was getting on with their drinking. Jerry was serving again, and she told herself that there'd be time later to put things right.

Hurrying outside, she put her hood back up and rushed to her car. Rain was falling harder than ever, hammering the car's roof as she opened the back door and leaned in to take a look.

"Mummy?" the little boy groaned, resting on a blanket on the back seat, barely able to lift his head to look at her.

"It's okay," she told him. "We're here. I've got the key."

***

Once the key had turned in the lock, Sally pushed the door open and then turned back to her son. She'd laid him down on the floor at the top of the stairs, and it took her a moment to gather him up and then carry him through into the dark, cold bedroom.

"It's okay," she said again, for what must have been the tenth time since she'd carefully lifted him from the car. "We're here, see?"

In the darkness, she could just about make out the single bed over on the far side of the room. She carried Tommy over and then she very slowly crouched down and settled him onto the bed, as rain dashed the window nearby. Taking care to not hurt him, she listened out for any hint that he was in pain. Or, rather, more pain than normal.

"How are you feeling?" she asked, as she reached over and switched on a bedside lamp. "Does it hurt?"

Wincing slightly, Tommy turned and looked across the room. His skin was a sickly yellow color, and his bloodshot eyes seemed to be having trouble focusing. A smattering of blood was caked around his lips, although Sally quickly took a tissue from her pocket and began to wipe the blood away.

"I'm sorry it took so long," she said, as roars could be heard coming from the bar area downstairs, "but I couldn't manage it any quicker and -"

Suddenly Tommy let out a gasp of pain and began to clutch his stomach.

"It's okay," she told him, reaching out and

putting a hand on his shoulder. "Listen to me, everything's going to be fine now. The hard part's over." As those words left her lips, she knew they weren't quite true, but she was desperate to make him feel better.

"There's only one bed," he whispered, still in a great deal of pain.

"I'll sleep on the floor."

"But -"

"Don't worry about that now," she added, moving one of the pillows down and then lifting his head, trying to make him more comfortable. She slipped the pillow into place and then gently lowered his head again. "Mummy's here, and Mummy's going to take care of everything."

Downstairs, another – louder – roar rang out.

"Is this the place?" Tommy asked, as another trickle of blood ran from the corner of his mouth. "Is this the place you told me about?"

"It is, honey," she replied, forcing a smile even as tears filled her eyes. "This is Crowford, and I promise you that now we're here, everything's going to be perfect. Forever."

# CHAPTER ONE

*Six months later...*

"SALLY!" ERIC SHOUTED FROM the door as he continued his slow, stumbling attempt to get outside. He'd already taken several minutes to get across the empty room, and he seemed to be constantly on the verge of falling over. "You're a diamond, girl!"

"Goodnight, Eric," she replied, drying a glass as she looked over at him. "Keep safe on the way home."

"I only live over the road," he pointed out as he stepped outside, although he managed to bump against the jamb in the process.

"Even that might be a little difficult," she

said, setting the glass down and heading over to the window.

Peering out at the dark street, she was just about able to make out the dark shape of Eric Garner shuffling across the road. She could see that he was searching for his keys in his pockets, and she waited until he reached his front door. Even then, she worried that he might topple over, so she watched as he pushed his front door open and lurched through. Finally, a moment later, the door slammed shut, and Sally realized that the old man should be fine.

"Did he make it without falling and bashing his head open again?" Matt Ford asked, glancing at her as he rolled a cigarette.

"He'll be fine," she replied, making her way back behind the bar. "Once he's inside, I think he just passes out in his armchair until morning. It's just that little journey across the road that causes him trouble from time to time. He's such a sweet man, though. It must be so hard for him, living all alone after his wife died."

"Mavis was a legend," Matt said with a faint smile. "She had the brightest blue hair you've ever seen, and – I kid you not – blue teeth."

She furrowed her brow as she finished drying some more glasses.

"Blue teeth?"

"Just a couple," he added, baring his own teeth and tapping at them. "On the side. And a pink one too."

"How does that work?"

"No idea. Never asked her." He lit the cigarette and took a drag, and then he pulled one of the ashtrays closer. "So Jerry's left you all alone again, has he? Where's the governor gone, anyway?"

"I have no clue," she told him. "It's fine, I know he likes to get as far away from the place as possible on his nights off. Most likely he won't wash back through the door until tomorrow. He tends to fall asleep on his friends' couches and sleep the night away. He usually shows up again around lunchtime."

"And you don't mind being here on your own?" he asked. "Overnight, I mean. In this big old creaky building."

She set the dishcloth down and headed over to him. Taking the cigarette as soon as it was offered, she had a drag and then passed it back to him.

"I like old buildings," she explained, glancing at the clock and seeing that it was almost time to shut the place for the night. She handed the cigarette back to him. "They've got a certain charm."

"You know," he continued, "if you're being brave and you really *are* scared here by yourself, I could always stay over."

"Thanks but no thanks," she said, rolling her eyes and taking the cigarette again. She had one more drag, before stubbing it out in the ashtray. "Time to go home, Matt," she added. "I want to get that door locked before Pat or any of the others from the club decide to pop in for one last drink on their way home."

"But -"

"And I'll be fine," she said firmly. "There's no ghost here. Really, there's nothing." She looked up at the ceiling and thought of the dark, empty rooms upstairs. "Not even one."

\*\*\*

Stopping at the top of the stairs, Sally kept the light off and stood in darkness, listening to the silence of the pub now that the customers had left and the building was all locked up.

>She waited, but she heard nothing at all.
>"Hey," she said finally, "are you here?"
>Silence.

Still keeping the light switched off, she stepped over to the door to her room. Her footsteps caused the old boards to creak slightly, but there was still no sign of any ghostly figure. She turned and looked over her shoulder, just about able to make out some of the other doorways at the far end of the landing, and then she pushed her door open and stepped through into her poky little bedroom.

She looked at the neat single bed in the corner.

"Hey," she said again, "if you're here, give me a sign."

Struggling to hold back tears, she waited, but she already knew that she was on a hiding to nothing. How many times had she crept about in the pub after closing, hoping that finally she might see or hear some sign that she wasn't truly alone? She wanted to call out again, but at the same time she was worried that she might end up scaring him. Then again, after six months, she was starting to wonder whether something might have gone wrong.

"Tommy," she whispered finally, "if you're here, there's no need to be afraid. It's Mummy, I just want to talk to you. I just want to see you."

Again she waited, and again the only response was the silence of the empty room.

Heading over to the bed, she sat down and

switched on the lamp, and then she picked up the framed photo that she always kept on the nightstand. She immediately felt tears in her eyes as she looked down at the shot of her son's happy, smiling face. The picture had been taken on his last birthday, right before he'd begun to feel poorly. The final months of his life had been spent in and out of hospitals, filled with various forms of chemotherapy as the doctors had tried desperately to save him. The cancer had eaten away at him from the inside, until eventually he'd died shortly after they'd arrived in Crowford.

And since then... nothing.

Every time Jerry went out for the night and left her alone, Sally tried to find some way to contact her son's ghost. She'd called out to him endlessly, she'd sat and waited in darkness for hours, she'd been so patient and still there'd been nothing. People constantly talked about ghosts that were supposed to be seen or heard in the pub, she'd heard so many variations of the same basic stories, but she'd experienced nothing at all and she was starting to think that the whole thing was just a fantasy.

And fantasies, she knew, had a tendency to crumble.

"Tommy," she said, as a tear ran down her

cheek, "I know it might be hard, or scary, but this is exactly why I brought you to Crowford. This town is supposed to be the most haunted place in the country, there are supposed to be almost more ghosts here than living people. I don't know why that's the case, and I don't really care, but..."

Her voice trailed off.

"Tommy, I just want to speak to you one last time," she continued finally, as a tear fell onto the photo's glass. "Just once, just so that I can tell you how much I love you, and how much I miss you. Can't you appear to me once, just to let me know that you're okay and that you're at peace? Because I've got to admit, I'm really starting to struggle here. I keep telling myself that you're around somewhere, but the truth is, I haven't sensed you once since you died. It's almost as if..."

She swallowed hard as she realized that sooner rather than later she was going to have to accept the truth. She'd been delaying that moment for so long, but she could feel a sense of dread and failure slowly creeping up through her chest, filling her soul and pushing away any last remaining hope. Finally, still holding the photo, she realized that she couldn't fool herself any longer.

"You're not here," she said, closing her eyes as more tears ran down her cheeks. "There are no ghosts in the pub at all. You're gone forever."

Sitting alone on the bed, in darkness, she began to sob. Her cries were the only sound, finally disturbing the brooding silence of the empty building.

# CHAPTER TWO

"YOU KNOW," MATT MUTTERED to himself as he stood in the hallway of his house and slipped out of his coat, "if you're being brave and you really *are* scared here by yourself, I could always stay over."

He paused, and then he sighed.

"Stupid!" he said as he hung his coat on the hook. "In what universe was a line like that ever going to work on a classy girl like Sally Cooper? Now she probably things you're a complete moron."

Catching his reflection in the mirror above the hall table, he stared at himself for a moment before sighing again. He tried to stand a little straighter, to fix his posture and pull his sloping shoulders back, but deep down he felt that he didn't cut a very striking figure. He took a moment to try to change his hairstyle, but this too already seemed like a lost cause. As for his shirt, which bore several small ketchup stains...

"And she'd be right," he added. "Face it, she probably has people asking her out all the time. Just 'cause she bums a cigarette from you occasionally, that doesn't mean she's interested. It just means she likes you as a friend and she feels comfortable around you. You should be happy with that, instead of trying to turn it into something else."

He leaned back against the wall and listened for a moment to the silence of the house. No matter how many times he tried to tell himself that there was no point pining after Sally, there was a stubborn little atom of hope that remained stuck somewhere in his mind, and he just couldn't shake the thought that maybe – with a little luck and an injection of charm – he might yet have a chance.

"Matthew?" a voice called out suddenly from upstairs. "Matthew, is that you?"

"Who else would it be, Mum?" he replied.

"Have you been at that pub again?"

"I just popped in for a couple of drinks," he explained. "I'm not drunk."

He waited, but he could already hear his mother shuffling around upstairs. Usually she'd be tucked up in bed by the time he got home, and he couldn't help feeling a flicker of dread in his chest as he realized that this time she seemed somewhat agitated. A moment later he heard the loud creak of the bed as his mother sat down. Evidently a day spent knitting and watching the television had failed to tire her out.

"Matthew?" she shouted. "Are you coming up? Bring me a glass of water!"

\*\*\*

"I've been talking to your father all evening," Jean explained as she settled back on the bed, "and he thinks you need to look for a better job. The mines -"

"I'm not talking about this again, Mum," Matt said as he set the glass of water on her nightstand. "I've made my decision, and I'm sticking by it. And Dad's not here, you know he's not."

"He was here just this evening," she told him, pointing at the foot of the bed, "sat right there. We talked for hours about all sorts of things! Including you!"

"Dad's been dead for nine years," he reminded her, struggling to hide the sense of irritation in his voice. "You know that. I took you up to his grave just the other day. We went with

Roger, remember?"

He waited for an answer.

"Do you remember that we put some flowers on his grave?" he added. "I got some nice ones from Tesco and we took them up there, you said it'd been too long and you were probably right. Roger brought some sandwiches, and later you told me you thought he shouldn't have eaten them there. But the thing is, Dad's gone. I mean, he's *really* gone. And he doesn't pop back to have chats."

"He's not happy with you," she replied, as if she hadn't heard a word he'd just said to her. "He thinks you need to get back down those mines, or you need to get work somewhere else. There's no in-between. Every day that you spend out there, shouting and causing trouble, is another day that makes it harder for you to get a new job. You can't afford to be picky these days, Matthew, there just aren't that many jobs around at the moment. Your father would be telling you the same thing. You're wasting your time."

"Dad would never say something like that."

"I know what he told me," she replied defiantly. "I was married to that man for thirty-seven years, I think I understood him a little better than you did."

Although he knew better than to argue with

her, Matt felt that he couldn't let her last point go. He'd been enduring his mother's constant criticism for months, and most of the time he'd bitten his tongue; lately, however, she'd started bringing his father into the discussion, claiming to have received messages from beyond the grave, and he genuinely felt as if he needed to put a stop to all the nonsense.

"Dad would be proud of what I'm doing," he told her. "Hell, he'd be out there with me every day, manning the barricades and -"

"Watch your language!" she snapped.

"You know I'm right," he continued, pointing toward the window. "He'd be out there with a placard, shouting louder than anyone else. How can you possibly say that he'd want me to be a strike-breaker?"

He waited, but she had no response and he was starting to think that perhaps he'd made his point. He looked down at the foot of the bed, at the spot where she'd started claiming to see his father, and for a moment he thought of the old man's smiling face. Although he desperately wanted to believe that his father's ghost might be lingering in the house, deep down he knew that there was next to no chance. A moment later, hearing a creaking sound out on the landing, he looked toward the door.

"Nothing good ever came of sitting around and doing nothing all day," Jean said grumpily. "The Devil makes work for idle hands, Matthew."

"I'm not idle," he replied, turning to her again. "I'm out there every day, I'm..."

Sighing, he realized that there was absolutely no point arguing with her. Instead, he stepped back from the bed and took a moment to calm down.

"I'm turning in," he told his mother. "Is there anything else you want before I go to bed?"

"I want lots of things," she grumbled. "I want a son I can be proud of."

"Goodnight, Mum," he replied, turning and heading to the door. "I might be leaving for the line a little bit earlier tomorrow, so don't worry, I can get my own breakfast."

"No, you can't," she said, as she rolled over and switched the lamp off, "I'll just have to be up in time, that's all. I'll have your breakfast on the table at six, how's that? And I'll have a lunch done for you as well. I still don't know why you bother going out there, though. It's not as if you're ever going to change anything."

He bristled, but this time he managed to keep from getting drawn into the same old argument.

"Goodnight, Mum."

He bumped the door shut and made his way across the landing, and then he hesitated as he looked back toward the bathroom door. Bathed in moonlight, the bathroom appeared almost to exist in another, softer world, and Matt couldn't help but think back to the very last time he'd ever seen his father, right before the old man had dropped dead after suffering a massive heart attack. They'd exchanged a few words about the football results, and then Matt had gone downstairs, only to hear a thump.

And that had been the end of Fred Ford; miner, war hero, dog-racing enthusiast. At least, according to Doctor Eymur, he hadn't suffered.

"Hey, Dad," he whispered now, just in case some sad swirl of mist might appear and briefly take his father's form. "You *would* agree with the strike, wouldn't you?"

He waited.

"I know you would," he added finally. "Mum's wrong. You're not appearing to her, you're gone, I know that. And if you were here, you'd be right behind me. In fact, if anyone was looking for your ghost and they came here, they'd be looking in the wrong place. You'd be out there on the picket line with me, not moping about the house." He paused. "I wish I could talk to you one last time," he muttered. "Or just see you. Just to know that you're around somewhere."

He waited a moment longer, in case his father's spirit might like to speak up and make a few points, and then he stepped into his room and pushed the door shut.

The landing was empty now, and dark, and silent save for a faint murmuring sound that could just about be heard coming from the master bedroom.

"I've tried to tell him," Jean was saying in the darkness, her voice heavy with sadness as the bed creaked again under her weight, "but will he listen to me? Of course he won't. He's just wasting his life away."

# CHAPTER THREE

THE FOLLOWING MORNING, SITTING in the cafe opposite the pier, Sally stared out the window and watched as a seagull tried desperately to gain access to a bin. Forgetting all her fears and worries, she kept her gaze fixed firmly on the bird as it pull on a scrappy edge of the bin-liner, and she waited to see whether or not its little plan might succeed.

"Okay, I need to work on my conversation skills," Jane said, sitting opposite her, "because there is no way I should be less interesting than a bloody seagull."

Startled, Sally turned and saw that her friend had returned from the counter with two fresh coffees.

"Sorry," she murmured, glancing out the

window again and seeing that the seagull was still working on the bin. "My mind was completely empty there for a moment."

"No kidding," Jane replied, pouring a sachet of sugar into her coffee and then giving it a stir. "You've been in a world of your own ever since you walked through that door. Come on, spill, what's wrong? Did a customer give you trouble last night?"

"No!"

"Then it's a guy. Have you got a date?"

She leaned across the table.

"It's not that Matt guy, is it? 'Cause he's a drip. You can totally do so much better than him."

"It's not a guy," Sally told her, before hesitating for a moment. She knew that she'd have to come out with the truth eventually. "I just came to a realization last night. About the pub."

"You realized that you could be doing something a damn sight more exciting than serving over-priced bad beer to a bunch of morons? What was it that tipped you off? Did someone get dared to eat a urinal cake again?"

"I realized that there's nothing there," she explained. "Not upstairs, I mean."

"I'm lost."

"It's not haunted," Sally continued. "You know how people always say that there's a little girl haunting *The Crowford Hoy*, or that there's some woman who used to live there and she appears sometimes, or that there's some other ghost? It's not true."

"What made you figure that out?"

"Time. And patience."

"Every pub in this town has a ghost story," Jane told her. "There's a gray lady in *The George*, and a spooky little girl in *The Crown and Anchor*, and apparently some famous painter haunts *The Old Bottle*. The point is, even the people who tell those stories don't necessarily believe them. The stories about *The Crowford Hoy* are pretty much the same, they're just fairy-tales told by excitable drunk people." She paused, waiting for Sally to reply, but she quickly realized that something else was wrong. "This is about Tommy, isn't it?"

"I didn't say that," Sally replied quickly.

Too quickly.

"It's been six months, hasn't it?" Jane continued. "Are you wondering why your son's ghost hasn't appeared to you?"

"I..."

Sally's voice trailed off.

"Can I ask you something?" Jane added. "I never quite understood why you packed up and rushed down to Crowford. It seems like you had a life in London, and a support network, and even after your separation from Tommy's father things don't seem to have been going too badly. I mean, I know people move across the country if a good job comes up, but did you really have to come all the way to Crowford – a town you have no ties to – just for a job working in a pub?"

"It's complicated."

"There weren't any pub jobs going in London?"

"I said it's complicated!"

Jane tasted her coffee, before starting to add another sachet of sugar.

"Or did you come here specifically because of something Crowford has to offer?" she asked.

"Like what?"

"Like a reputation for hauntings," Jane suggested, watching Sally's face carefully, waiting for any sign that she was on the right track. "I'm trying to be delicate about this, but... How long after you arrived here did Tommy die?"

"About an hour."

"Literally right after you got here?"

"I carried him into the room upstairs in the pub," Sally explained, feeling a shudder pass through her chest as she thought back to that awful night, "and I set him on the bed. I talked to him for a few minutes, and then I went to fetch a couple more bags from the car. By the time I got back up, he was gone."

"That must have been so awful."

"I knew he didn't have long," Sally admitted. "I thought he might last at least a few more days, though. I thought I'd get to take him to the beach and show him the sea, thinks like that."

"Were you rushing him down here because you wanted to make sure he died in Crowford? Because you thought that'd make it more likely for him to come back as a ghost?"

Sally looked out the window and saw that the seagull had managed to pull out more of the bin-liner, which was now trailing in the wind, although the contents of the bin remained elusive.

"It sounds so stupid now," she whispered, with tears in her eyes. "From what I read about Crowford, it's like everyone who dies here comes back as a ghost. Well, not everyone, but a lot of people. And I knew Tommy was coming to the end, even if I didn't want to admit that to anyone, or to myself." She turned back to Jane. "Is it so bad that I wanted to find some way to still see my son? Even if I knew that it was a desperate attempt, is it so bad that I at least thought I could give it a try?"

"You wouldn't be the first person to do

something like that," Jane told her. "I've heard similar stories before, of people coming to Crowford because they think they can take advantage of its... reputation. So what happened to make you finally give up on the idea?"

"Last night I just sat in my room and realized that the entire place was empty." She leaned back in the plastic chair. "I uprooted him for nothing. I put him through all that trauma of the car journey... for nothing."

Jane tested her coffee again, and immediately grabbed a third sugar sachet.

"You know, Sally," she said cautiously, "I *do* believe in stuff like that. I've lived in Crowford my whole life, I know what it's like to be aware of things happening on the edge of your perception. When we were kids, we used to go out to the old abbey in the forest, and sometimes we'd go to look through the windows into the old school house, or we'd sit on the beach until midnight, convincing ourselves that ghostly sailors were about to appear. The point is, I never saw anything definitive, but I always felt as if some kind of presence was just out of sight."

She paused.

"I also know what it's like to want to see someone again. I lost my sister, remember?"

"But you've never seen her ghost?"

"Nope," Jane said, with sadness in her voice. "That doesn't mean that it's impossible, though."

"Maybe not," Sally replied unconvincingly. "I'm just starting to think that I might be better off starting again. I came to Crowford for something that turned out to be all in my head. Now it's like I'm the one who's haunting the place."

"I get how you feel," Jane said. "You know, someone once told me that even if a place is haunted, sometimes the ghosts... settle."

"Settle?"

"Like, if they're not disturbed for a while, they kind of forget themselves. They drift away, and even though they're still there, they're much more passive and much harder to notice. They just start fading into the background until they might as well not exist at all."

"Okay, but how does that help?"

"Well, she told me that sometimes all you have to do is stir them up a bit."

"Now *I'm* the one who's starting to get lost," Sally replied.

"Are you working tonight?"

"For a change. Seventh night in a row. It's okay, though, I don't mind, and I definitely need the money."

"And Jerry's gonna be out on one of his all-nighters again, right?"

"Almost certainly. Why?"

"I'm gonna pop over around closing time," Jane told her, "and we'll see if we can kick-start things a little. Don't ask me any more than that, because I'd feel stupid trying to explain it, but just trust me here. Assuming you *want* to kick-start anything, that is."

"You mean you think you can force the ghosts to appear?"

"It's a bit more subtle than that," Jane replied. "It probably won't work, but at the very least we can have a bit of fun. What do you say? Are you up for one last try?"

"I suppose so," Sally said, even though she was struggling to summon much enthusiasm. Deep down, she'd begun to accept that there was no hope left. "We just have to make sure that Jerry doesn't find out, because he's definitely opposed to any mention of ghosts. It's the one thing that's guaranteed to make him angry."

"He'll never find out," Jane told her. "It won't even take that long. I promise you, though... if there *are* any ghosts in that pub, any at all, we're going to find them tonight!"

# CHAPTER FOUR

"LOOK WHO IT IS!" Nigel said with a grin, as he watched Matt making his way across the field. "Little Matt Ford has finally decided to show his face!"

"I was over at the Lark Road entrance," Matt explained, looking ahead and spotting the usual police officers blocking the way. One of them was his uncle, Roger Ford. "I took a short-cut across the golf course to get here."

"My wife used to work at that golf course," Nigel told him. "Back in the sixties, Sheila was a waitress. And do you know what? She had to wear a pink bunny costume, and she had to be topless while she served the drinks."

"Shut up, man," one of the other strikers said with disdain. "No-one wants to think about your Sheila topless."

"So what's going on here?" Matt asked, craning his neck to get a better view of a few more strikers on the other side of the road. "Any developments?"

"What do you think?" Nigel asked. "No-one's tried to cross the picket line this morning, if that's what you're wondering. Other than that, we're all out here freezing to death and waving these bloody signs while businessmen and politicians hundreds of miles away ignore us." He paused for a moment. "I hope you don't mind me saying this, Matt," he added cautiously, "but you don't half look like your old man this morning."

"I'll take that as a compliment," Matt muttered, looking past the crowd and seeing the pit headgear in the distance. "We should be down there working, not standing around here like idle buggers."

"Blimey," Nigel said with a chuckle. "Now you *sound* like old Fred too."

\*\*\*

One hour later, having taken his leave of the strikers at the Arlish Road entrance, Matt trampled across another field, aiming to complete a full route all around the edge of the site. He wasn't entirely sure why he was making this particular journey; he simply couldn't stomach standing still all day on the line, yet he also wanted to stay as close as possible to the action. Now, stopping at the edge of the field and looking down the hill, he had a perfect view of the colliery as it lay still and unused.

"There's enough coal down there for another hundred years," he remembered his father telling him once. "There's no reason for anyone to close the place in our lifetimes."

Now those words echoed to him through the years, and he couldn't help but wonder what his father would think if he could see the state of the pit now.

Shoving his hands into his pockets, he turned to walk away, but then he froze as he suddenly heard the unmistakable sound of the pit's machinery starting up. Glancing over his shoulder, he told himself that he had to be wrong, but sure enough he realized he could see figures down there on the site itself, seemingly getting back to work. He watched, stunned, but he knew that the only possible explanation was that somehow the strike had been called off. After all, a few men might have crossed the lines, but he could see hundreds down there now.

He began to make his way back across the field, determined to find out what had happened, but at that moment he saw that a man was standing nearby, watching the scene with a curiously satisfied expression on his face. Clearly very old, leaning on a cane and wearing a dark coat with a hat pulled down to almost cover his features, the man seemed utterly oblivious, even as Matt changed direction and began to make his way closer.

"Hey!" he called out, waving at the man. "Do you know what's going on?"

Stopping, he began to realize that it was strange for him not to have noticed the man just a moment earlier. After all, he'd made his away across the field and he felt sure that he'd have spotted anyone else within half a mile or so. Besides, the man looked to be in his sixties, perhaps even older, and Matt figured that he most likely couldn't move very fast.

"Excuse me," he said cautiously, worried about spooking the man, "I don't mean to trouble you, but do you have any idea why the pit's started up again?"

This time the man began to turn to him, although not all the way. A curious smile crossed the man's lips, and he kept his gaze fixed on the distant colliery.

"Is the strike over?" Matt asked. "Did they bus men in from somewhere else to get it going again? Please, if you know, you have to tell me."

"What are you talking about?" the man replied.

"The colliery," Matt continued. "There's

been a strike for months, and I didn't hear anything about it being broken today. But now everything's moving again and I just don't understand how."

"I think you might be mistaken," the man suggested. "Nothing has changed."

"But..."

Matt turned to look back down at the colliery, and in that moment the sound of the machinery came to an abrupt halt. There were no men visible down there now, nor was there any sign at all that the pit was back up and running. Feeling for a moment as if he was on the verge of losing his mind, Matt tried to figure out exactly what had just happened, but he knew that he'd definitely seen activity.

"I think I might be going mad," he said finally, turning to the man again. "I saw... I mean, I swear..."

"You saw the place running at full pelt?" the man asked, raising an amused eyebrow.

"I didn't just see it," he explained. "I heard it too. There must have been a couple of hundred men down there, they can't all have vanished!"

"No," the man replied, "I suppose they can't. In that case, exactly where do you think they are now?"

"Is this some kind of trick?" Matt asked. "Is someone trying to make us go nuts, so they can swoop in and shake it all up?"

"I'm not sure that I follow how that would work," the man told him. "Exactly who do you think would be able to orchestrate something on such a grand scale? Not to mention, how would they sneak so many men onto the site, when all the entrances and exits are being watched by members of the strike? The idea simply makes no sense whatsoever."

"I know that," Matt said, looking over at the colliery again, "which is why I don't get it. It was as if, for a few seconds, everything just went right back to how it was before."

He watched the scene for a few more seconds, lost in thought.

"Oh," the man said suddenly, furrowing his brow, "I'm terribly sorry, I think I... Yes, I mistook you for someone else."

"For who?"

The man simply stared at him. Matt turned to look at the colliery again, then back at the man.

"Is it -"

Stopping suddenly, he realized that he was all alone. He turned and looked around, but the elderly man – who'd seemed so frail and had barely been able to stand – had disappeared in the blink of an eye.

"Hello?" Matt called out, but he already knew that he was all alone.

He looked back over at the colliery, but the

site still appeared dead and unused. Whoever those people down there had been, and whatever they'd been doing, they were gone now and Matt couldn't help but wonder whether they'd really been there in the first place. Sure, it was technically possible that they'd all ducked into one of the main buildings while he hadn't been looking, but that explanation wasn't exactly very likely. He knew that ghosts weren't real, however, so on balance the most likely explanation was simply that – in a moment of madness – he'd imagined the whole thing.

After glancing around one more time to look for the old man, Matt turned and hurried back across the field.

\*\*\*

"Great," Nigel said as he spotted Matt returning to the picket line a short while later, "just when you think things can't get any worse. What are you doing back here?"

"Just checking to see what's going on," Matt said uncomfortably.

"Been on another of your perimeter wanders, have you?" Nigel asked. "I don't know why you bother, lad. Come across anything interesting this time?"

Matt hesitated for a moment, but he knew he'd only be laughed at if he told anyone about what he'd seen.

"Nothing," he said.

"Are you sure? You look a bit pale there, son."

"I'm fine," he replied, keen to cut down any further discussion. "So what's the plan here? If no-one's coming or going, who's even going to know that we're protesting here today?"

"That's not the point," Nigel replied, nudging him in the ribs. "You know that. We're here to make a stand, and we're also here to make some noise. So how about less sight-seeing and more protesting?"

As those words left his lips, another police car slowly drove around the corner. The other strikers all began to jeer, and Matt – not wanting to seem as if he lacked conviction – joined in and started shouting too.

## CHAPTER FIVE

"JANE," BRADLEY SAID AS he opened the door to his bedroom, "what do you want?"

"I need to borrow something," she told him, pushing the door open and stepping past him. "Man, you could open a window every now and then, this room reeks."

"You know, you could always ask instead of just barging in."

"I knocked, didn't I? If you've really got a problem with it, you should see about getting that lock fixed."

Picking her way across some piles of clothes, she made her way to the window and pulled the curtains open, letting midday light flood into the room. She turned and looked around, and for a moment she could only stare at the complete mess that covered every inch of the floor. Carrier bags full of old food packets had been left piled on the bed, and a home computer was running on the desk. The room was filled with so many books and old clothes and bags of 'stuff', there was barely any room for a human being to fit.

"What do you *do* on that thing all day?" she asked him, peering at the computer's screen.

"I'm learning to write computer code," he replied, somewhat defensively. "Computers are the future, Jane. One day everyone'll have one."

"I won't," she told him. "I'm not that pathetic."

"One day you won't be able to live without one."

"You really believe that kind of stuff, don't you? How... cute."

"Just because this is a shared house," he said with a sigh, "doesn't mean that you need to share your opinions on everything that goes on in it. What do you want?"

"Something I saw in here once," she replied, climbing over the bed and dropping down on the other side, next to the desk. "You know, Bradley, this time your hoarding might actually come in useful. Do you happen to have everything categorized, or is it a case of fumbling around until you find what you're looking for?"

"You're not borrowing anything."

"Relax. If I'd just come in when you weren't here and taken it, you'd never have noticed it was gone."

"That's not the point!"

"You're just panicking because you're not used to having a girl in your room."

"That's so not true."

"No self-respecting girl would ever want to be in a room like this," she told him.

"*You're* here."

"Not for sexy times, Bradley. Besides, do I actually strike you as the self-respecting type?"

She pulled some boxes out of the way.

"Careful!" he snapped.

"What? Am I going to mess up your very elaborate filing system? Give me a break."

"This is my room," he said again. "You don't see me storming into your room, do you? Even before you fixed the lock on your door."

"And if you've never tried to go in there, how to you know about the lock?"

"That's not the point," he replied, although now he seemed more awkward than ever.

"Gross!" she added, holding up a pile of dirty magazines. "Is this what you do with yourself in here all day, Bradley? Will being able to write computer code ever help you get an actual girl who doesn't have staples in her belly?" She let one of the magazines fall open, revealing one of the naked models. "You don't get stuff like *that* on a computer screen, do you?"

"Maybe one day," he suggested.

Setting the magazines aside, she pulled a couple of bin bags out of the way and then began to rifle through a pile of board games. After just a moment, she spotted what she was after and began to wriggle it out from the very bottom of the pile.

"I'm not giving you permission to take anything!" Bradley said firmly.

"Then I'll steal it."

"No. You've got no right to be in here! I ought to go to Mr. Sullivan and complain!"

"Bet you don't."

Once the box was free, she stood up and turned to him so that he could see the front.

"A board for contacting the dead?" he said, raising a skeptical eyebrow. "What do you want with one of those?"

"That's none of your business, Bradley," she replied. "I only need it for one night, just to do some light contacting of the dead, and then I'll have it back to you first thing tomorrow. It won't get damaged in any way. Do we have a deal?"

"What do I get out of this?"

"Absolutely nothing other than my undying gratitude," she replied, clambering back across the mess and heading to the door, where she stopped next to him. "There are some very disgusting-looking socks under your bed, Bradley. I think they might be the primary cause of the smell. If you clean the place up a bit, I might be tempted to stay a little longer next time I come into your room. We could chat, maybe have something to eat, and you could show me a little bit of that computer coding that keeps you busy all day. Maybe. Think about that."

She poked him in the chest, and then she carried the board over to the stairs.

"That's my private property!" he called after her. "I don't give you permission to damage it in any way!"

She turned back to him.

"Does it come with instructions?"

"A friend of mine made it a few years ago," he told her. "She was trying to come up with some new way of talking to spirits, something a bit different. Of course it doesn't come with instructions."

"Do you know how to use it? Beyond the obvious, that is."

"Not really."

"Okay, but *are* there rules?" she continued. "Come on, Bradley, you know everything! You must know something about this! Why do you even have it if you're not interesting in how it works?"

"I just thought it looked cool."

"You're tragic," she told him. "You know

that, right? Really tragic."

"I'm pretty sure you're supposed to be careful with those boards," he added. "Not that I believe in any of that stuff, of course. It's clearly nonsense designed to titillate immature minds. But if you *do* believe in all that ghost rubbish, then you should definitely not just start messing about with a board like that. People who believe in it tend to think that there can be very serious consequences if you do it wrong."

"Huh." She looked down at the board for a moment, before shrugging. "Can't be that complicated. I've seen them being used in movies. Catch you later, dude!"

\*\*\*

"Seems easy enough," she muttered a short while later, standing in the kitchen and moving the marker across various letters on the board. "Talk to a ghost, get it to move the thingy, work out the message. Job done."

She continued to play with the marker for a few seconds.

"Spirit, I summon thee," she continued with a faint smile. "Man, there has to be more to it than that."

For a moment, she tried to think back to any horror films she'd seen that included a spirit board.

She understood the basics of how they worked, but she couldn't shake the feeling that there might be certain special words that she was supposed to use.

"Spirit, are you here?" she asked. "I don't know, is that enough? Spirit, I conjure thee and demand that you talk to me and..."

Her voice trailed off.

"Whatever," she added with a sigh.

She set the marker aside, before heading to the fridge and grabbing a carton of orange juice. She took a swig straight from the carton, which she then placed back in the fridge. With her eyes still fixed on the spirit board, however, she couldn't help but wonder whether the stupid thing might actually work. It wasn't exactly like the ones she'd seen in films; rather, it seemed to have only a few letters and numbers on its surface, along with various other symbols.

Then again, contacting the dead wasn't exactly the primary purpose of her plans.

Making her way over to the chair in the corner, she sat down and took the receiver from the phone. She looked through the address book on the shelf, and then she dialed one of the numbers. She waited, and after a few seconds she heard somebody pick up on the other end of the line.

"Hey," she said, "it's me. Jane O'Neill. I know I told you I'd ring on Saturday, but I've managed to get things into gear a little quicker than

I planned."

As she listened to the voice on the other end of the line, she twirled the phone cord with her fingers and looked back over at the spirit board.

"Did you put the money in my account?" she asked. "Because I'm going to pop down to the bank later and check. I'm not doing anything until I know that you've kept up your side of the bargain."

She smiled as she listened to the voice.

"Everything's going according to plan," she continued after a moment. "Don't worry, I'm certain that by this time tomorrow, I'll have exactly what you want."

She listened for a moment longer.

"No, I told you not to worry," she said firmly. "It's all going to be taken care of. I promise you, Sally doesn't suspect a thing."

# CHAPTER SIX

"YOU REALLY *DO* LOOK like him, you know."

Turning, Matt saw that Nigel Winter had wandered over from the bar. Having followed the other strikers to the social club at the end of the day, Matt had intended to only have half a pint, but instead he'd found himself looking at all the old photos on the wall. Glancing back at one particular set of pictures, he saw his father's face grinning in a black and white image.

"Fred Ford was a good man," Nigel continued. "One of the best I ever knew. If he was here now, he'd be telling us exactly how to handle this strike."

"Are you sure?"

"Why wouldn't he?"

"It's just that my mother..." Matt's voice

trailed off for a moment. "Forget it. Sometimes I think she's losing her mind."

"Your father always said that men should stand for what they believe in. For what they think is right, you know? He said that if we all did that, the world would be a better place. He also said that all the other stuff would figure itself out in the end, but that you'd always be able to live with yourself if you knew that you'd done the right thing."

"I suppose that makes sense," Matt replied, although he still couldn't shake a sliver of doubt. "I just can't help wondering what he'd be saying right now about everything that's going on in Crowford."

"Can't ask the dead for their opinions," Nigel pointed out as he turned to go back over to the bar.

"Wait, who's that?" Matt asked, spotting a familiar face in one of the other pictures. Stepping closer, he saw a black and white shot of his father standing next to the man he'd met earlier. He reached out and pointed at the man's face. "Do you know who that guy is, with Dad?"

"That's old Ernest Dwyer," Nigel told him. "He's something of a local historian, he takes a keen interest in anything to do with the past of Crowford. If you go in any of the bookshops in town, you'll usually find some of his work. Pubs, the mill, the mines, local incidents and disasters... you name it, Ernie's probably written a book about it. In fact, come to think of it, he's about the right age to have maybe served in the war with your old man. He doesn't get out much these days, though." He glanced around, to make sure that he wasn't about to be overheard, and then he leaned closer. "Some folk say that he got into quite an argument with those Grace sisters, and you know what vindictive old cows they can be."

"Do you know where I can find him?" Matt asked.

"Haven't got a clue, I'm afraid," Nigel said, before taking a long sip of beer and then wiping his lips. "I heard he keeps himself to himself of late. He might live up the old mill end, but I'm not even sure about that. Shame, really. He used to be such a big part of the town."

Left alone in front of the photos, Matt couldn't help but think back to his encounter with Ernest Dwyer earlier near the colliery. He was certain that the man had simply vanished into thin air, even though he knew that wasn't possible. In which case, he was starting to think that he needed to track him down and try to figure out exactly what was happening out beyond the picket line.

\*\*\*

"Matthew?" Joan called out as soon as he opened the front door. "Is that you?"

"It's me, Mum," he replied, offering his customary greeting. He didn't know why she ever bothered asking; it wasn't as if anyone else ever entered the house.

"Have you been at that club again?"

"I popped in for a quick half, yes," he said, bristling at the thought that he had to explain himself. "It's not as if -"

"I don't know what's up with young men these days," she said, interrupting him as she set a saucepan on the hob in the kitchen. "Drinking all the time, it's not good for you. I was talking to your father just this afternoon and he told me he's not happy with you, my boy. He wants you to get down to town first thing in the morning and start looking for a new job. He says there must be hundreds of cards in the exchange, all you've got to do is pick a few and make some phone calls."

"Dad wouldn't want me to leave the strike," he replied, as he wandered through and saw that she was making beans on toast for supper. "You weren't talking to him this afternoon, Mum. This is all just stuff that's in your head."

"He thinks you're wasting your life away," she continued. "You're twenty-eight years old and you should have a trade under your belt by now."

"I'm a miner."

"Mining's going to be a thing of the past soon. Haven't you listened to the radio lately? Give it five years, the pits round here won't be open anymore. You want to get a head-start and find a good job before all those other layabouts start flooding the market. Soon there'll be a few hundred young men looking for work and you need to make sure that you stand out from them. You don't want to end up taking the dregs and doing something like sweeping the streets."

"You don't know what you're talking about," he said under his breath, before letting out a loud sigh. "Dad was eight when his parents moved the family down here from Yorkshire. They came because they wanted a better life, and because they heard a place like Crowford might be the future. That wasn't even that long ago. It's too soon for us to be giving up now."

"Your father doesn't think so."

"Dad's dead."

"He was in here with me all afternoon," she added sniffily, "and he thinks -"

"He's dead!" Matt shouted suddenly, shocking himself with the outburst. Even as his mother turned, horrified, to look at him, he realized that he could no longer contain his anger. "You're just telling me what *you* think," he continued, "and trying to glorify it by pretending that Dad agrees with you, when the truth is he's been dead for almost ten years now and he's not coming back! And no matter what you might think, there's no way you can dredge him up and act like you know his opinion!"

"How dare you speak to your own mother like that?" she replied, clearly shocked by his tone. "Young man, you might be nearly thirty years old but you're still my son and I won't be spoken to like that in my own home! You were raised better!"

"I was raised to know the difference between what's real and what's just fantasy," he told her, "and I won't let you pretend that Dad disapproves of me, because I know that's not true!"

He waited for a response, but she merely took some bread and slipped the slices into the toaster.

"Raising your voice to your own mother," she muttered after a moment. "Whatever is the world coming to?"

He opened his mouth to reply, but he already knew that there was no point arguing with her. Looking over at the dining table, he saw that his father's usual chair had been pulled out, almost as if his mother actually believed that he'd come back for a natter. A part of Matt desperately wanted to make her understand that she was deluded, but he also knew that she missed his father terribly, and he couldn't quite bring himself to shatter her beliefs.

"How many slices do you want?" she asked as the first two pieces of toast popped up.

"I'm going out," he murmured, turning and

heading back to the door.

"What do you mean? Your supper's ready!"

"I'll get something on the way," he told her, desperate to escape from the house, at least for a few hours. "I'm sorry, I remembered something I have to do. Oh, and by the way, there's nothing wrong with sweeping the streets. If no-one did it, you'd soon be complaining."

Without giving her time to argue, he grabbed his jacket and headed back outside. He pulled the door shut and stopped for a moment, trying to work out where to go, and then he hurried off toward Cobham Street. He wanted to go somewhere he could be left alone, somewhere he wouldn't bump into anyone he knew, so he figured he'd try one of the pubs on the very far edge of town, maybe even out in one of the villlages beyond Crowford itself. And he told himself that by the time he got home later, he'd have made a final decision about whether or not to continue with the strike.

# CHAPTER SEVEN

"LOOK, THAT'S NOT WHAT I meant," Barry said as he sat at the bar in the Crowford Hoy and tried to get his point across. "All I'm trying to say is that Robson's no step up from Greenwood. If we want to really make an impact at the next cup, we need to come up with something new, and I reckon it might be time to consider having a foreign manager."

As a murmur of disapproval rang out, Jane turned and looked over at Sally.

"Is the conversation in here always this scintillating," she asked, "or is it just my lucky night?"

"You'd be surprised how much football knowledge I've picked up while I've been working here," Sally told her. "Can you believe, I actually have an opinion about the qualifying format for the next set of games in Mexico?"

"You're becoming one of them," Jane said disapprovingly.

"Listen," Sally replied, stepping over to her while the football conversation raged nearby, "I've been thinking, maybe tonight isn't such a good idea after all."

"What do you mean?"

"I mean that it feels wrong somehow to start messing around with things we don't understand."

"Are you kidding?" Pulling the box out from her bag, she set it on the bar. "Call it a spirit board, or a marker board, or whatever, but do you have any idea how hard it was for me to get hold of this thing?"

"Where *did* you find it, anyway?"

"I had to go into Bradley's room."

"That's brave of you." Sally turned the box around so she could see the front. "I don't know, it just gives me the heebie-jeebies to see the thing. What if we're messing with something we should leave alone?"

"Are you scared?"

"I'm nervous, I'll admit that." She sighed. "All I'm saying is that it might be best to just accept that there's nothing here."

"And I'm telling you, that a pub this old is *bound* to have a few ghosts. We just need to give the atmosphere a bit of a stir, that's all, and wake them up." She paused. "You want to contact Tommy, don't you?"

She waited for an answer, but she could tell that Sally was uncertain.

"You told me that's the whole reason you rushed him to Crowford when he was dying."

"It was, but now I'm not so sure," Sally replied. "What if the right thing to do is just walk away? What if Tommy doesn't want to appear to me?"

"Why wouldn't a young boy want to see his mother one last time?"

"I just -"

"What've you got there, love?" Ralph asked, leaning over and peering at the box. "What's a spirit board?"

"None of your business," Jane said, sliding the box out of sight and turning to grin at him. "Shouldn't you be talking about football or cricket or whatever else you guys use to fill your empty lives?"

"No need to be like that," he muttered, turning away from her. "I was just being friendly."

"We're doing this," Jane told Sally firmly, holding the box up again. "It's natural for you to have doubts, and I totally get that, but you'll thank me later. Trust me, once this pub closes and we've got the place to ourselves, we're going to use this board and we're going to see if your son's ghost is here. That's what I'm here for, to keep you going in moments of doubt." She reached over and put a hand on Sally's shoulder. "And because I'm your best friend."

*** 

"Goodnight, guys," Sally said as Percy, Ralph and the others traipsed out of the pub a little after 11pm. "Take care on your way home. Don't do anything I wouldn't do."

She heard a few grumbled replies, and she smiled as she made her way around the bar and headed to the door. After pulling the blind down, she turned the key in the lock and checked to make sure the door was secure, and then she wandered over to the window and leaned down to check that the main outside light was off. Once she'd done that, she realized that she was delaying the inevitable, and she heard a faint bumping sound as she turned and saw that Jane was already setting the board out on one of the tables.

"You know," she said cautiously, "I can't even be sure that Jerry won't be back tonight. He usually stays out, but if he happens to come home early, he's really not going to be happy about what we're doing."

"So?"

"So he's my boss, and he could sack me."

"Jerry's not capable of sacking anyone," Jane suggested. "If he sacked you, he'd have to do some work himself. Now, get me a pint of whatever lager's coldest in this place, and then get your bum over here and onto a chair. We need to get started."

Sally opened her mouth to suggest once more that they should rethink their plans, but she knew that it was always impossible to argue with Jane. Although they'd only met a few months earlier, shortly after Sally's arrival in Crowford, she was already grateful for Jane's constant determination to push through and get things done. Even though the spirit board made her feel uneasy, therefore, Sally figured that she had little choice but to go along with the plan.

"If you told me I'd do one of these things one day," she said as she headed back around the bar, "I'd have thought you were nuts. I've seen them in films, but to be honest I wasn't even sure that they really existed."

"Oh, they exist," Jane said, taking care to put all the pieces out in the right positions. "My gran had one when I was a kid. I was never allowed to play with it, of course. She always said it was for adults only."

"So do you know the rules?" Sally asked.

"There aren't any."

"I'm pretty sure there are."

"In films, maybe," Jane continued, "but

come on, this is real life. You just use the marker thing to see if any ghosts want to deliver a message. If they do, great. If they don't, you do a few shots and have a laugh." She paused as she watched Sally pouring a couple of pints. "I think this might really help you, though. Don't take this the wrong way, Sally, but sometimes I get the feeling that something's really weighing heavy on your mind. It's almost like you're holding something in."

"You mean when I get a kind of vacant look on my face?" She smiled. "That's just when I'm genuinely not thinking about anything."

"I'm serious," Jane told her. "You use humor to mask it, but I know that deep down you've got serious issues. Doing this board tonight might help you face those, even if it doesn't mean that you directly make contact with Tommy. Which you totally will do, anyway."

"Maybe."

Jane watched her for a moment longer.

"Don't you *want* to make contact with him?" she asked finally. "Despite everything you've said, are you having genuine second thoughts?"

"Of course not."

"Because if you really hate the idea, I can pack it up. I suppose I'm just wondering why you'd be having all these doubts..."

Sally glanced over and stared at the board for a moment, as if she was truly considering the possibility.

"No," she said after a few more seconds, "we should at least give it a try. I mean, you went to all this trouble already."

"Damn straight," Jane told her. "To be honest, I don't think there's much else to do except dim the lights a little and get started."

"Shouldn't there be more of us," Sally asked, carrying the drinks over.

"How do you mean?"

"In every film I've ever seen," she continued, setting the drinks on the table, "there are at least three people around the board."

"Sure, but where are we gonna find a third person?" Jane asked. "It's late, and I'm not even sure where we'd find someone we trust. Come on, it might not be perfect, but at least we can give it a try. And I really don't see how any ghost would turn us down just because we're a person or two short."

"I just worry that it might not work if we don't do it properly," Sally told her.

"You're stalling," Jane said firmly. "After all this time, tonight's the moment of truth, Sally. Are you going to be brave and really see if you can contact Tommy, or are you going to chicken out and spend the rest of your life wondering?"

Sally opened her mouth to reply, but then – staring down at the board – she realized that her friend might have a point. She hesitated for a moment longer, and then she took a seat.

"Excellent," Jane said, sitting opposite her and reaching out to touch the marker with one finger. "Let's get this show on the road."

# CHAPTER EIGHT

"I THINK THAT'S A *no*," Sally said an hour later, as she and Jane looked down at the marker that they were touching with one finger each. "Listen, this was a nice try, but -"

"We're not giving up yet," Jane said firmly. "This sort of thing just takes time."

"It's gone midnight," Sally pointed out. "Aren't you tired?"

"There's something here," Jane said, looking around the empty bar area, "I can feel it. It's just that we need to draw it out a little more, that's all. Why don't you start by telling me a little more about Tommy?"

Sally sighed.

"You need to stick with it," Jane added. "Listen, go and grab us each another beer and then we'll push on. If we haven't managed anything by one, maybe we'll call it a day, but I'm not quitting yet and neither are you!"

"Whatever you say," Sally replied, grabbing their empty glasses and heading to the bar. "I'm not doubting you, and I'm very grateful to you for making the effort with me, but I just feel that if anything was going to happen, it would have happened by now."

"This was never going to be easy," Jane said, reaching down into her bag and tilting it open. She glanced at the tape recorder and saw that it was still running. "Hey, tell me about the night you and Tommy arrived here. I know this might be painful, but it also might stir some memories a little and encourage him to come out. What was it like on the night he died?"

"I don't know that I want to go into that too much."

"But you want to talk to him again, don't you?"

"We haven't heard any sign that anyone's here," Sally pointed out as she finished pouring the first pint. "This building's easily a couple of hundred years old, and we haven't heard so much as as creak or a groan. Shouldn't the place at least settle at little at night? There's been nothing."

"Maybe we should try upstairs," Jane muttered, glancing at the ceiling. "Maybe we should try in the room where he died. Don't you think it makes sense that his spirit would be closer there?"

She turned to Sally and watched as she finished pouring the drinks. For a moment, feeling a little sorry for her friend, Jane wondered whether she should simply cut the night short and admit defeat. After all, she could always argue that her payment was for the attempt, and that she'd never guaranteed results. Then again, she didn't want any complications, and she felt that she was close to getting what she needed. As Sally carried the drinks back over, she decided that she was simply going to have to hurry things along a little.

"Tell me about Tommy," she said, "and -"

Before she could finish, they both heard a bumping sound at the pub's front door. They turned and looked, just as the handle wiggled, and a moment later the letterbox flapped open.

"Hello?" a familiar voice called out.

"Is that..."

Sally hesitated.

"Sally, are you in there?" Matt continued. "Hey, I can see you. Are you having a lock-in? Can I come in?"

"What the hell's that idiot doing here?" Jane asked.

"Hang on," Sally replied, heading over to the door, "I'll get rid of him."

"If you're having a lock-in, it's only right

that you let me join you," Matt said as Sally crouched down to look at him through the letterbox. "Hey, Sally. Please, I don't want to go home right now, I've been out all night and the light's still on in Mum's bedroom. I really don't think I can handle another argument with her right now, and she's been on fine form over the past couple of days. Can you do me a favor and let me hang out here for a while?"

"We closed an hour ago," she pointed out.

"But you're still open."

"No, we're just... talking."

"Are you playing a board game?" he asked, peering toward the table.

"No, we're -"

"That's one of those spirit boards!" he added. "Hey, what are you guys up to? Are you trying to contact the dead?"

"Matt, please just go home," she replied, "and do me a favor, don't mention this to anyone, okay? Especially not to Jerry."

"Is it just the two of you in there?"

"Matt -"

"Because that's never gonna work," he added. "You know you need at least three people, right? Have you even invited the spirits properly?"

"We..."

Sally's voice trailed off, and then she turned to look at Jane again.

"We can manage," Jane said firmly, clearly irritated by the interruption. "Matt, I mean this in the nicest possible way, but leave us alone."

"I've used one of those things before," Matt explained. "When I was a kid, I mean. Listen, I'm not saying I believe in them, 'cause I don't, but if you want to have even a slight chance of making it work, you need a third person. There's no way you'll get in touch with anything if there's only two of you."

"You don't know that for sure," Sally told him.

" Cross my heart and hope to die."

Sally hesitated, before looking at Jane again.

"Well?" she asked. "Is he right?"

"I don't know," Jane said cautiously. "Maybe. Technically. It's not like this thing came with a handbook."

"I'm not drunk," Matt said. "I walked all the way out to *The Cock* at Wimbourne, which took me over an hour, I had one drink and then I walked to *The King William* and had a drink there, and now I'm here. I've walked miles tonight and I've only had two pints, so I'm completely sober." He waited for an answer. "Listen, if you're just playing around and trying to spook yourselves a little bit, then knock yourselves out and I'll jog on. But if you actually want to have even a chance of getting in touch with any spirits, then you need to do a few things differently, and you need a third person."

He waited again.

"It couldn't hurt to try," Sally told Jane.

Jane opened her mouth to reply, but then she held back. Gritting her teeth, she looked at the letterbox and saw Matt staring back at her, and then she sighed.

"Fine," she muttered, as she reached into her back and checked the tape recorder again, "I guess one more person can't hurt. Even if he *is* the dullest man in Crowford."

"Sounds like you're in," Sally said, getting to her feet and unlocking the door, then pulling it open so that Matt could enter. "Just remember that if Jerry comes home early, you and Jane are going to have to scarper fast."

"I'm used to leaving places quickly," he told her. "A misspent youth taught me that particular skill."

Sally took a moment to lock the door properly, and then she followed Matt across the room.

"Jane," Matt said as he reached the table, "always a pleasure."

"Likewise," she replied unconvincingly. "I hope you're not going to crack bad jokes and hit on Sally all evening, because this is actually a serious endeavor."

"This board looks pretty old and basic,"

Matt said, looking down at the set-up on the table. "That's not necessarily a problem, though. Do you have anything that might provide a physical link to any of the spirits that you're trying to contact? I don't know exactly what ghosts are supposed to haunt this place, but something – anything – connected to them would help. Is it an old landlord or someone who used to live here?"

He looked at Jane, then at Sally, then at Jane again. He furrowed his brow, and then he slowly turned back to Sally.

"Is it a specific person?" he continued.

"Kind of," Jane murmured.

"If it's a specific person," he explained, "you can really boost your chances if you have something they owned, or even just something that was around when they were alive. Can you rustle something like that up?"

Jane looked over at Sally.

"Yeah," Sally said cautiously, "I mean... I can find something."

"That'd be really useful," Matt told her.

"I'll go and..."

Sally's voice trailed off. She seemed uncertain, even as she made her way to the hallway behind the bar and began to go upstairs.

"Don't take this the wrong way," Matt said, turning to Jane, "but so far it looks like this whole séance attempt has been a little on the amateur hour side of the scale. You're lucky I came along."

"Yeah," Jane said, forcing a smile before pulling a pack of cigarettes from her bag. "Whatever would we have done without you?"

# CHAPTER NINE

OPENING THE LITTLE BROWN suitcase that she'd pulled out from under the bed, Sally felt a shudder pass through her bones as she saw her son's clothes neatly folded away. She hadn't looked in the suitcase since the night they'd arrived in Crowford, and tears were filling her eyes as she spotted his old Superman t-shirt.

"Pull yourself together," she whispered under her breath as she moved a few more t-shirts aside and saw what she was looking for.

Holding up a light brown stuffed bear, she thought back to all the nights Tommy had clung to the bed when he was afraid of the dark. She'd almost had him buried with his favorite toy, but at the last moment she'd decided to hang onto the bear for sentimental reasons. Now she was starting to regret that decision, thinking that Tommy would have liked to have his bear with him for the cremation. For a few seconds, she couldn't help but think of her son's body in the coffin as the flames began to burn through the wood.

"Maybe I can give him back to you tonight," she said, sniffing back more tears. "So you never have to be alone again."

\*\*\*

"A toy bear?" Matt said as Sally placed Mr. Bear on the table, next to the board. "That doesn't even look very old. Who did it belong to?"

He waited for an answer, and finally the penny dropped.

"Wait," he said cautiously, "are you trying to contact..."

Again, he waited for one of them to say something, and then he pulled his chair away from the table.

"I think this is a bad idea," he said firmly. "I know I was all gung ho about it earlier, but that was before I realized you were trying to contact..."

He watched Sally for a moment, but she could only stare at the bear as she struggled once again to keep from crying.

"Sally," Matt said cautiously, reaching over and putting a hand on her arm, while trying to figure out the right thing to tell her, "I think this might be too much for you. Didn't your son die right here in this pub, just after you arrived?"

She nodded, keeping her eyes fixed on the bear.

"Why didn't I realize sooner what you guys were doing?" he continued, before turning to Jane. "Did you really think this was a good idea?"

"Sally wants to talk to him," Jane replied matter-of-factly. "People do it all the time, they try to talk to dead relatives. Why shouldn't she try to get a sense of closure?"

"Sure, but..."

He turned to Sally again.

"We can stop," he told her, "and -"

"No," she replied through gritted teeth.

"It's just that -"

"We've come this far," she continued, before taking a deep breath. "If you're not comfortable, Matt, I understand that and I won't blame you for leaving, but we're going ahead. I know you said there need to be at least three people, but that might not be true, we might be able to get through to him anyway if you tell us exactly what to do." She turned to him. "I don't want to force you to do anything that makes you feel bad."

Matt tried for a moment to think of a diplomatic way he might back out, but deep down he knew that by doing so he'd be condemning the exercise to failure. As much as he wanted to spare Sally any unnecessary pain, he also figured that if she was really sure about contacting her son, he could try to make that happen for her.

"There's no guarantee this'll work," he told her.

"I know," she replied, "but I really need to at least..."

She paused.

"If we get in touch with him," she continued, "would there be any way for me to... talk to him in private? Would you guys be able to leave the room for a few minutes?"

"Wouldn't that jeopardize things?" Jane said, looking over at Matt. "I mean, if we break the circle or whatever, would the ghost stay or go? I just think it'd be an unnecessary risk." She turned to Sally. "Don't worry, you can say anything you need to say to him, and none of it will ever leave this room. I promise."

"Anything's possible," Matt told her.

"Should we just get on with this?" Jane asked, glancing at the clock on the wall and seeing that it was already almost one in the morning. "I'm not being funny, but some of us need our beauty sleep. Besides, I have to be up at seven for work so I'm already kinda guaranteeing that I'll be exhausted all day."

"Are you really sure?" Matt asked Sally.

She thought for a few seconds, and then she nodded.

"Jane's right," she said, reaching out and adjusting Mr. Bear for a moment so that he was sitting up properly. "We should get started. One way or the other, I want to know if this has a chance of working."

\*\*\*

"I'm asking again," Matt said as they sat in silence, each touching the marker with one finger, "if there's any spirit here who wants to speak to us. Don't be afraid, anyone at all, just come forward and give us a message."

They all waited, but the room remained silent.

"This still isn't working," Sally said after a moment.

"Be patient," Matt replied. "We're doing everything right, but these things take time. There are lots of reasons why a spirit might not make itself known immediately."

"You think there's a shy ghost here?" Jane asked, before turning to Sally. "Why don't you tell us again about the night Tommy died?"

"I don't think that'd help right now," Matt said.

"To be fair, you don't seem to know very

much about all of this," Jane replied, turning and glaring at him. "We've followed your advice and we're no better off than we were before so why don't we try a new approach? There's no harm in bringing a little raw, honest emotion into the -"

Suddenly they all heard a faint creaking sound coming from somewhere upstairs. They looked toward the ceiling and waited, but now silence had fallen once more.

"It's probably just the building settling," Jane said nervously.

"It wasn't settling before," Sally pointed out.

"Yeah, but if a ghost heard us," Jane continued, "then why would it respond by taking one step across a room upstairs? That doesn't really make a lot of sense if you think about it logically. What kind of ghost would decide to communicate by hopping once in a random empty room?"

"The needs of the spirits are beyond our understanding," Matt told her.

"Bullshit!" she snapped. "People don't suddenly become ridiculous just because they're dead!"

"Can we just focus, please?" Sally asked. "Jane, this was your idea in the first place. Matt might be right, we might just need to give it a little more time."

"I still think talking about Tommy would help," Jane grumbled. "It might, you know, stir things up a little. I mean, if the little guy is anywhere around, he might like to know that he's remembered. Doesn't that make sense to anyone else?"

"Is there anyone here?" Matt asked, looking around the room. "Is there anyone who wishes to speak to us?"

He hesitated, and then he turned to Sally.

"Wait, your surname's Cooper, right?"

She nodded.

"So your son -"

"Yeah. Thomas Cooper. Tommy. We actually didn't notice until after we'd agreed on it, and by then the name had kind of stuck and -"

Suddenly she looked down at the marker as it began to slide across the board toward the word Yes.

"Who's doing that?" she asked.

"Not me," Matt said. "Jane?"

"I'm not doing anything!"

All three of them watched as the marker stopped on Yes. For a few seconds, no-one dared ask another question.

"Now would be a really bad time for anyone to be messing about," Matt said, with fear in his voice.

"I said it's not me!" Jane snapped. "I know that's what you were both thinking."

"What do we do now?" Sally asked.

Matt hesitated, before looking around the room. The far end of the bar area was shrouded in darkness, but he watched for a moment just in case he was able to spot any movement. When he looked back down at the marker, he realized that he hadn't really, truly considered the possibility before that they might actually succeed in making contact with the dead. Now his throat felt dry, and he had to force himself to continue.

"Spirit," he said finally, "are you the ghost of Sally's son Thomas Cooper?"

They all waited.

After a few seconds, the marker slowly slid across the board until it was over the word No.

# CHAPTER TEN

"NO!" JANE GASPED, PULLING away and stumbling to her feet, then backing across the room. "No way! Which one of you assholes did that?"

"We didn't do anything," Matt told her. "Quick, get back here, we need you."

"No chance," she said keeping her eyes fixed on the board. "One of you just wants to screw with me, that's all. I could feel it, someone was moving the damn thing!"

"If it wasn't Tommy, then who was it?" Matt asked, turning to Sally.

"This building's at least three hundred years old," she pointed out, trying to stay calm. "A lot of people must have lived here over the years."

"And died here," he pointed out.

"Will you two stop talking about this crap?"

Jane yelled, clearly on the verge of a full-blown panic attack. "You're not gonna convince me, you know! I'm not so stupid that I can be tricked by some kind of cheap stunt!"

"We have to find out who it was," Matt said, reaching a hand toward her. "Jane, you can't leave now, not while the board's still open."

"You're not tricking me again," she replied, grabbing her bag before taking another step back. "You know what? It's been fun, guys, but I'm out of here."

"You can't leave while it's open!" Matt called after her.

"Yeah? Well watch -"

Suddenly a loud thud rang out, and Jane spun around and looked over toward the bar.

"What was that?" she asked, her voice filled with terror.

"It wasn't the building settling," Sally said, "that's for sure."

"We need to stay calm and do this properly," Matt told them. "You can't just open a board and initiate contact, and then run away, that's not how it works." He turned to Jane. "We have to see this thing through to the end now."

"It's not real," she stammered, still watching the bar.

"Then you won't mind coming back over and joining in again, will you?" he suggested.

"This wasn't supposed to actually work," she said with tears in her eyes, as she turned to look at Sally. "I'm sorry, I know you probably hate me for this, but all I wanted to do was give you closure and help you talk about Tommy. I mean, the dead can't actually come back, they..."

She paused, and now tears were running down her face.

"They just can't," she added. "*Can* they?"

"I understand how you feel," Sally replied, "but please, whatever we're in the middle of, we have to finish it."

Jane hesitated, still clutching her bag, before looking back down at the board on the table.

"It's your board, isn't it?" Matt continued. "If you take it home while it's open, there's no telling what might happen. There are rules about this sort of thing, Jane. Whether you believe that we've contacted a spirit or not, either way, we need to get this done. You've got to finish what you started."

"This is so stupid," Jane said, before slowly making her way back over to the table and retaking her seat. She set her bag down, and then she looked at the board. "I swear, if I catch either of you moving that thing deliberately, I'm going to kill you."

"Let's just get it over with," Sally said, putting a fingertip on the marker, followed a moment later by Matt. "Please, Jane..."

Jane reached down and checked that the recorder in her bag was still running, and then she placed a finger against the marker and waited.

"Well?" she said, unable to hide her sense of agitation. "You heard the woman."

"We mean you no harm," Matt announced, looking around the room once more. "Spirit, are you still here?"

Before the last word had even left Matt's mouth, the marker shot across the board until it was over the word Yes.

"I don't like this," Jane said through gritted teeth.

"Spirit," Matt continued, "can you tell us your name?"

They all waited, but this time there was no response.

"My name is Matthew," he said, "and these are my friends Sally and Jane. We only want to know who we're speaking to. Can you tell us your name?"

Again, they waited in vain.

"Why wouldn't it tell us its name?" Jane asked. "That doesn't make any sense."

"There's no harm in telling us who you are," Matt pointed out. "Please, we just wanted to talk to you."

They waited, and this time the marker

finally began to move again, scraping across the board until it had scratched out the letter W.

"E," Matt read out loud as the marker to make cuts in the wood, "A... V... E..."

"Weaver," Sally said suddenly, just as the marker finished creating the letter R. "There was a landlady here called Weaver. Margaret Weaver, I think, or something like that." She paused, trying to remember. "No, Mildred. Mildred Weaver."

In that instant, they all heard another loud knocking sound over by the bar. They turned once more, watching the shadows in case they spotted any hint of movement.

"Jerry has a collection of old documents relating to the pub's history," Sally said, "and there's that plaque on the wall with all the old landlords listed." She turned to Matt. "Should I go and take a look?"

"Be quick."

Getting to her feet, Sally made her way around the bar. She switched on the lights at the far end of the room and stopped in front of a wooden plaque containing a list of names.

"Mildred Weaver," she read out loud after a few seconds, "was the landlady here from 1919 to 1947. For the first three years, she ran the place with her husband Leonard, and then I guess he died and she carried on alone. That's twenty-eight years she spent here in total. I've never heard anyone mention what she was like, but I wouldn't mind betting that a few of the regulars might remember her."

"That doesn't help us now," Matt pointed out, as Sally headed back over to the table. "We need to know exactly who this is."

They all touched the marker again.

"Is this Leonard or Mildred Weaver we're talking to?" he asked.

He waited.

"Is this Leonard?"

The marker moved to the word No.

"Is it Mildred?"

The marker moved to the word Yes.

"Is she actually here right now?" Jane asked, looking around. "Is she invisible but standing right here, reaching down onto the table?"

"Can we ask her about Tommy?" Sally said. "I mean, does it work like that? Would she know about any other ghosts in the pub?"

"Do you know Tommy?" Matt continued. "Thomas or Tommy Cooper. Have you met him here at all?"

This time, they received no answer.

"She might not consider the question to be important enough," Matt suggested. "I've heard sometimes that they can be like that. It takes effort for them to communicate and they're only willing to make that effort if they have a good reason. Then again, that means she must have wanted to talk to us once she realized she had the opportunity. It's not easy trying to figure out how a ghost's mind works."

He turned to Sally.

"We can still get her to help us, but I think first we need to make the connection stronger."

"Whatever it takes," she replied.

"Are you sure about this?" Jane asked. "Can't we just keep trying to get in touch with Tommy?"

"Unfortunately, I think while Mildred has the mic, we need to go through her," Matt explained, before looking down at the marker again. "Mildred... I mean, Mrs. Weaver... I don't know what you prefer to be called, but I'm assuming you're talking to us because you think we can help you with something. Please, tell us what you want."

They waited, and this time the marker began to shudder slightly while remaining in one place on the board.

"What does that mean?" Jane asked.

"I don't know," Matt replied, "it's almost like... I almost feel like she's angry. Does anyone else get that?"

"Ask her again," Sally said.

"Mrs. Weaver," Matt continued, "we want to try to help you, but first you're going to have to tell us what you want."

Jane looked around, terrified in case she

might spot some sign of the ghostly woman.

Suddenly the marker began to move again, although this time it was much slower, grinding against the top of the board almost as if it was being pushed down way too hard. A couple of times it briefly stopped, but some unseen force kept it going until it stopped and they saw that a single letter had been scratched into the surface.

"A?" Sally said.

The marker moved again, creating another scratch in the wood.

"N," Matt said.

This was followed by the letter N again, then I, and finally the marker scratched the letter E.

"Annie?" Sally whispered, looking at each of the others in turn before glancing at the board again. She hesitated, and then she raised her voice. "Who the hell's Annie?"

In that instant, the board flipped up off the table and flew straight past her face before slamming against the wall and then dropping to the floor.

"Whoever she is," Matt said, swallowing hard, "I don't think Mildred's a big fan."

## CHAPTER ELEVEN

"ANNIE," SALLY WHISPERED, KNEELING in front of a trunk in one of the upstairs rooms, going through Jerry's collection of old documents and photos related to the pub's history. "Why does that name seem so familiar?"

The trunk contained a huge collection of postcards, photos, newspaper clippings and papers, some of them stretching back over a hundred years. While that was all very useful, Jerry's haphazard storage methods meant that everything was jumbled together; although he'd been talking for year about writing a book about the pub's past, Jerry had never managed to get past the information-gathering stage, so Sally felt as if she was searching for a needle in a haystack.

Still, Jerry had occasionally gone on long

rambling digressions about the pub, and Sally was certain that she'd heard the name Annie mentioned a few times. She quickly realized, however, that Jerry hadn't been very selective when it came to his collection; the trunk contained everything from old newspaper adverts to receipts for beer deliveries that had taken place back in the 1950's, and actual photos – not to mention anything with names – were few and far between.

Finding a small batch of pictures, she began to look through them, but all she saw were shots of people from the distant past. Most of the photos appeared to show customers going off on charabanc trips from the pub, although there were a few photos of people relaxing in the garden. Shots of the pub's interior, meanwhile, showed that not much had changed over the years, but that wasn't much help to Sally as she continued to search for some mention of Mildred Weaver or – even better – of the elusive Annie.

"Come on," she muttered under her breath, turning some photos over, hoping to find notes that might mention someone named by that name, "there has to be something in here somewhere. I just have to find it."

***

"None of this makes any sense," Jane said angrily

as she sat at the table downstairs, tearing at a beer mat with her fingers. "Why would the ghost of some old landlady want to find someone named Annie?"

"I can think of plenty of reasons," Matt replied as he poured himself another pint. "Do you think I look good behind a bar? Do you think it could be a new career for me?"

"I think that beer's got more foam than a nightclub in Southend," she said snarkily. "Don't you think there's a danger that we're letting our imaginations run out of control? I mean, Sally's clearly very invested in what's happening here, so what if – and I don't mean this in a mean way – but what if she's been subconsciously moving that damn thing because she can't bear to accept that her kid's gone?"

"You're the one who set this whole thing up."

"That doesn't mean that I thought a ghost was really going to appear," she told him, before setting her bag on the table and reaching inside for a pack of cigarettes. Her hands were trembling slightly as she grabbed her lighter. "I mean, apart from people who are completely out of their minds, who actually believes in ghosts? Do *you* believe in them?"

"Maybe," he replied, thinking back to the strange man he'd seen earlier in the day.

"Sometimes."

"Okay, but that just proves my point, because you're a complete idiot." She rolled her eyes. "The point is, how could I be expected to think that an actual ghost might show up? The idea's ludicrous. Once people are dead, they're dead. They don't come back." She paused, staring into space for a moment. "They can't."

"Can I bum one of those?" Matt asked.

"No, sorry. I need them."

"All of them?"

"Yep. Sorry."

Sighing, he grabbed another pint glass from the shelf.

"Can I pour you a drink?"

"That you may do," she told him, "but I'm sick of beer for tonight, it's too gassy. Pour me a large glass of red wine. And I mean *large*! To the brim."

Getting to her feet as she lit the cigarette, she slipped her lighter into her pocket and headed for the back door.

"Where are you going?" Matt asked.

"Where do you think, moron? I need to get some fresh air. But you'd better have that glass of wine waiting for me when I get back inside, okay? And make it something nice, not that cheap crap he always tries to offload on people. Rioja, that'd be great. Ta muchly."

After sliding the bolt across, she pushed the door open and stepped outside. The night air was bracing, but she told herself that she really needed to escape from the pub's weird atmosphere. As she took a drag on the cigarette and looked out into the darkness of the Hoy's garden, she realized that her carefully-laid plans were starting to unravel. All she needed was to get Sally talking about Tommy, and to make sure that she had a few key sections of the conversation recorded on tape, and then everything would be fine. That had seemed so easy at the start, and she'd hoped that the spirit board would be the catalyst for finally getting Sally to open up.

And then Matt – stupid, dumb, lovesick, dopey Matt – had arrived and ruined everything.

She glanced back into the pub and saw that Matt was taking a look at the plaque on the far wall. Feeling a shudder pass through her chest, she realized that she genuinely loathed the man; at the best of times, he was something of a wet blanket, but at that particular moment he was jeopardizing her big payday. Sure, she figured she could still get Sally to talk, but the job was taking so much longer and she was starting to think that she might not get home until sunrise.

Disgusted by the sight of Matt, she made her way across the decking and stopped at the railing that separated the top part of the garden from the longer, grassy area. She still couldn't see anything down at the garden's far end, but after a moment she realized she could hear a faint scratching sound coming from the storage shed nearby.

She listened, telling herself that the sound had to be caused by some kind of animal, but she was feeling sufficiently shaken to need proof. After glancing around again, she headed over to the steps and down to the shed, and then she clicked her lighter and pulled the shed's door open to look inside.

"Gross," she said, as she saw cobwebs everywhere, along with several large spiders hanging in wait. "Does he *ever* clean this place out?"

The scratching sound continued, although now she was starting to realize that it was coming from behind the shed rather than inside. She shut the door and stepped around to the side, and then she crouched down and held the lighter out so that she could see into the gap between the shed and the wall.

The lighter cast a dancing circle of light against the shrubbery, and as Jane leaned closer she was starting to think that perhaps she was wasting her time. The area behind the shed carried a certain rotten aroma, one that deterred her from poking about too much. The last thing she wanted was to encounter more spiders. And then, just as she was about to get back up and head inside, she heard a rustling sound getting closer.

She looked behind the shed again.

"Hey," she said cautiously, "is anyone -"

Suddenly a shape lunged at her from the darkness, knocking her back with such force that she dropped both her lighter and her cigarette. In the momentary madness, she cried out as she felt sharp teeth scratching across her body, and then something large and furry slammed into her face before scrambling down onto the grass.

Startled, she turned and watched as a badger scurried away across the garden.

"Are you kidding me?" she gasped, sitting up and touching the side of her face, feeling the scratch-marks left by the animal's claws. "I'm going to need a tetanus shot after this!"

Shaken and trembling, she re-lit her cigarette and got to her feet. She was feeling a little faint, and after a moment she couldn't help but realize that the badger had left a foul smell on her clothes. Looking down, she saw that her jeans were torn and that one side of her shirt had been torn open.

"Damn you!" she snarled, turning and looking back over at the spot where she'd last seen the badger. "If I ever get my hands on you, I'll throttle you! I hope you get culled!"

Still muttering to herself, she turned and began to make her way back to the pub's back door.

She took a much-needed drag on her cigarette, and then – looking up at the pub's upper windows – she suddenly froze.

A little girl was standing at one of the windows, staring down at her.

## CHAPTER TWELVE

"HEY," SALLY SAID AS she heard someone step into the room to join her, "I'm really not having any luck in here. It looks like Jerry kept pretty much everything, but it's completely uncategorized."

Holding up, another receipt, she sighed.

"I'm all for keeping records," she continued as the footsteps moved closer, "but I really wish he'd done more to sort out the photos, and to try to identify the people in them. I mean, it's the people who are the heart of the place, right?"

She looked at another photo.

"Right?" she added.

She turned to see whether it was Matt or Jane who'd entered the room; to her surprise, however, she realized that she was all alone, even though she'd definitely heard footsteps approaching from behind. She looked the other way, but she knew without a shadow of a doubt that there was no way somebody could have hidden away so quickly. A flicker of fear ran up her spine as she realized that she might not be quite alone after all.

"Is anyone there?" she whispered.

Silence.

"Mrs. Weaver?" she continued, before another possibility crossed her mind. "Annie?"

She waited.

"Tommy?"

No.

She told herself to stay focused.

Hearing a click, she turned and looked over to the window. The sound had already ended, but it had been clear and distinct and there was no way she could dismiss it as nothing. She waited in case it returned, and then she slowly got to her feet and wandered over to the window. The air near the window was noticeably colder, but she figured that was just caused by some gaps in the old frame.

Looking out at the pub's back garden, she was just about able to make out Jane down on the decking, staring up with a somewhat bewildered expression.

Sally smiled and waved at her, and then – receiving no response – she turned to go back to the trunk.

Stopping suddenly, she saw that several

photos from the trunk were in the process of dropping onto the floor. She had no idea how they could have been moved from the interior, but she felt certain that she hadn't left anything balanced on the trunk's side. Making her way over, she knelt down again and began to take a look at the photos, which all showed black and white images of the pub's bar area from long ago.

Flicking through the shots, she hesitated as she saw one that showed several people standing at the bar itself, posing with smiles for the camera. The picture was clearly old, quite possibly from a century earlier, but there was nothing particularly noteworthy about any of the faces and there was certainly no sign of any women or girls who could be the elusive Annie. She checked the other pictures, and once again she found that she was out of luck.

"Come on, Jerry," she said under her breath, "how can you have done all this work without actually identifying anyone? You're always going on about how much you care about the pub's history."

A moment later, feeling as if she was being watched, she looked back across the room. The sensation persisted, although she still couldn't quite figure out the source. Then, just as she was about to turn back to look at the trunk, she realized she could see somebody watching her through the gap between the door and the hinges.

"What the -"

In a flash, the figure turned and ran, but Sally was already certain that it had been a young girl. She stumbled to her feet and raced across the room, stopping once she reached the landing. She looked around. There was no sign of anyone, but the door to Jerry's bedroom was open and she felt certain that it had been shut when she'd made her way upstairs earlier.

"Hello?" she said cautiously, making her way over to the door and looking into the dark room. The first thing she noticed was a distinct aroma of cheap cologne, but she was fairly sure that wasn't caused by any ghost. "Is anyone here?"

She waited.

No response.

"Annie?" she continued, thinking back to the figure and realizing that it had seemed to be a young girl. "Hey, is there anyone named Annie in here?"

Again, she waited.

Again, she heard nothing.

"It's okay," she said, taking a step into the room and turning the light on. There was still no sign of anyone, but she once again felt as if somebody was close. "My name's Sally and I won't hurt you. I only want to know what's going on. I can help you, if..."

As her voice trailed off, Sally realized with

incredulity that she was actually attempting to negotiate with a ghost. Figuring that the little girl had seemed scared, she told herself that she had to find some way to connect with her, to make her feel a little more safe.

Stepping over to the bed, she looked around again.

"It's okay to be scared," she continued. "Everyone gets scared sometimes, but you just have to be brave and face up to whatever it is that's upsetting you. And it's always easier to do that when you've got a little help. That's what I'm trying to do right now. I'm trying to help you and -"

Suddenly hearing a scratching sound, she turned and looked over her shoulder. The sound continued, and she realized after a moment that it seemed to be coming from over near the door, possibly out on the landing. She made her way over to look, but as soon as she left the room she realized that the sound was now coming from somewhere over her shoulder. She stepped back into the room, still trying to figure out exactly what was happening, and then she turned and looked at the door as she finally realized where the sound was coming from.

She hesitated, before reaching out and taking hold of the door, which had been left wide open with its handle bumped against the wall.

As the sound continued, Sally began to

slowly pull the door open, even as the scratching became louder and more furious. She was worried about finding someone standing behind the door, but she forced herself to pull it all the way, and then – as the sound abruptly stopped – she let out a shocked gasp as she saw that a word had been scratched into the wallpaper:

DON'T

Staring at the word, unable to believe that it could possibly be real, Sally tried to figure out some way that it might have already been there. Sure, the rest of the room was neat and tidy, and she happened to know that Jerry had redecorated just a couple of years earlier, but she told herself that it was vital to keep from jumping to conclusions. Just because she didn't understand why the word was on the wall, or why she'd heard the scratching sound, that didn't mean that a ghost was responsible.

Reaching out, she ran her fingers against the torn wallpaper. As she did so, however, she felt something brush against her elbow.

Turning, she saw that she was once again alone. She looked all around, watching the shadows in case she might have a chance of spotting any hint of movement, but there was nothing.

"If you're here, you have to prove it right now," she said, backing against the wall, looking across the room and waiting for some sign of the little girl. "I mean it, if you're here, show yourself. Come on, I'm not scary, I'm just trying to figure out what's going on. My name's Sally Cooper and if I can help you, I will. I just need to know what you want first."

She hesitated, before making her way through to her room. She looked at the bed, but at that moment she realized she could hear the scratching sound again.

Turning, she looked back out onto the landing and saw that another word had appeared on the wallpaper:

DON'T LET

"Who's doing that?" she asked quickly, trying not to panic.

She stood in silence for a moment, before stepping back into the room. As soon as she was behind the door, she heard the scratching sound continue. Although she wanted to go out and see what was happening, she forced herself to instead try to peer through the gap between the door and jamb. Finding that she couldn't quite see around far enough, she listened as the scratching continued for a few more seconds, before finally silence returned.

She waited for a few seconds, and then she cautiously made her way back out onto the landing.

She felt a shudder in her chest as soon as she saw the completed message on the wall:

    DON'T LET HER FIND ME

## CHAPTER THIRTEEN

"GREAT," MATT MUTTERED AS the beer tap began to run dry, leaving only a few more drops to fall into his half-empty glass. He tried the handle a couple more times, before setting the glass aside and heading over to the door in the corner.

After fumbling for a moment with the latch, he pulled the door open and looked down into the pub's dark, cold cellar.

"I'm just going to change a barrel!" he called out.

He waited, but Sally was still upstairs and Jane was still in the garden, so he wasn't too surprised to receive no response. The cellar wasn't entirely appealing, and he knew he could just switch to a different beer, but he figured he might as well have the one he wanted. Besides, changing the barrel didn't seem like it'd be too difficult, and he couldn't resist the chance to practice his pub skills. The possibility of having to start a new career was weighing on his mind and he felt that running a pub might be one of the better options.

"I'm just going to change a barrel," he muttered to himself, somewhat surprised, as he flicked a switch on the wall. "Little old me, a guy with absolutely no experience in the pub game whatsoever, is going to attempt to do something that even seasoned landlords sometimes completely screw up."

A light flickered to life at the bottom of the rickety wooden steps, and as he began to make his way down Matt couldn't help but worry that the steps might collapse under his weight at any moment. He told himself to stop fretting about the tiniest little things, and as he reached the bottom he was more worried about the fact that the cellar was so cold. He stepped around the corner and saw the kegs all lined up, connected to the various lines, and he spotted some more kegs pushed up against the wall.

Stepping over, he took a moment to locate a keg of Bloody Gunpowder No 9, which everyone with any taste knew was the finest ale produced by the Hayes and Storford brewery. It was at that moment, however, that he realized he had no idea how to properly tap a keg, although he'd heard plenty of stories about people doing it wrong. He'd always laughed at those stories before; now, however, he was starting to think that there might be a little more to the job than simply switching a few hoses over. In fact, he wasn't even sure where to start.

Spotting a keg that looked to have perhaps been tapped already, he made his way over and began to examine the top section, which he supposed was the part that he needed to attach to the lines. He spotted a couple of valves, and he picked one at random to try turning. When this failed to produce any obvious result, he tried the other, but this too did nothing. He stepped around the keg and crouched down, at which point he spotted another valve. Figuring that he might as well try to learn something, he gave the valve a quick turn.

In an instant, beer began to blast out at him, spraying him in the face. Panicking, he pulled back and then ducked out of the way, before somehow managing to reach around and close the valve.

"Okay," he said as he got to his feet again and wiped beer from his face, "I guess that's not the best start. What's a guy got to do around here to get a little -"

Suddenly the light switched off, plunging the cellar into darkness.

"Seriously?" he said, looking over his shoulder and seeing just a faint hint of light on the far wall, at the foot of the stairs. "Hey, did one of you turn that off? Would you mind turning it back on again? Some of us are trying to learn down here."

He waited, but nobody replied.

"I'm in the cellar!" he continued. "This place is like a death-trap, can you at least turn the light back on so I can get out?"

Looking up at the ceiling, he figured that the bulb might simply have failed. He knew that meant he'd never be able to try changing the barrels now, so he turned to head back upstairs.

Stopping immediately, he saw a silhouetted figure standing in the middle of the room, seemingly looking straight at him.

"Hey," he said, "you nearly gave me a heart attack."

He waited, but after a few seconds he began to realize that this figure was neither Sally nor Jane. Something about the stature and height seemed all wrong, although he was just about able to tell that the person appeared to be a woman.

"Okay," he said cautiously, "hi there, I don't know who you are but I just came down here to change a barrel. If you need proof, you can ask Sally, she should be right upstairs."

When the figure failed to respond, Matt realized that he could feel a niggling fear in the pit of his stomach, a sensation that was slowly starting to rise up into his chest. He thought back to the spirit board, and to the apparent communication with a woman named Mildred Weaver, and he tried to figure out who else might have randomly entered the pub over the previous few minutes.

"So I'm just going to go back up now," he continued, trying to plot the best way back to the steps, ideally one that would take him all the way around the edge of the room without having to go near the figure. "Feel free to stay down here, I really don't mind."

He took a step to the right, but in the darkness he failed to notice a bucket on the floor. He flinched as the bucket clanged and tipped over, and he hesitated for a moment as he kept his eyes fixed on the dark figure that still stood just a few feet away.

"Sorry about that," he muttered, before turning to head once more to the steps.

"Where is she?" a woman's voice asked suddenly in the darkness.

Stopping, Matt turned to her.

"I'm sorry?" he asked, trying to hide the fear in his voice.

The figure tilted its head slightly to one side.

"Where is she?" she gasped, and now her voice sounded even more frail and rasping than before. "You must know."

"I don't have a clue what you're talking

about," he replied, taking a step to the side, hoping to edge toward the steps while keeping her talking. "That's okay, though, you can just hang out down here and relax or do whatever it is that you came down here to do, and I promise that no-one'll disturb you."

He bumped against a bench, but this time he kept going. Glancing over at the steps, he realized that he was close, but he didn't want to risk running, not yet.

"Enjoy yourself, then," he added, turning to the figure again, "and try not to -"

Stopping suddenly, he realized that she was gone. He looked around, convinced that she must have simply made her way over to a different part of the cellar, but there was no sign of anyone. Although he couldn't see into the darkest corners at the cellar's far end, he figured that there was no need to go hunting for the figure. He hesitated for a moment longer, just in case anything stirred, and then he turned to go to the steps.

"Where is she?" the old woman snarled, standing right in front of him and then grabbing his throat, pushing him against the wall.

"Stop!" he gasped, trying to get free, even though her grip was far too tight.

The woman leaned closer, and now Matt was able to see her angry, lined face. Her skin was pale, although dark, deathly shadows hung under her eyes as she opened her mouth to reveal black, rotten teeth.

"Sally!" Matt tried to call out, although he was barely able to make a sound as he felt the woman's hand crushing his throat. "Someone! Help!"

"You'd do well to answer my question," the woman sneered, as her foul breath filled Matt's nostrils.

Unable to breathe, Matt reached up and tried to pull the woman's hand away. Her flesh was icy, and her skin was flaking in places, as she held him tighter than ever. Stunned by her strength, Matt fought for a moment longer to break free, and then he tried to push the woman back.

"Please," he groaned, "don't hurt me. I don't know what you want, but I didn't do anything wrong! Please..."

"I've waited long enough," she replied, as black blood began to run from her mouth, dribbling down onto the rough concrete floor. She leaned even closer. "Where is Annie Ashton?"

## CHAPTER FOURTEEN

"OKAY," SALLY SAID AS she hurried down the stairs and then made her way through into the bar area, "something really freaky just happened to me upstairs, I think -"

Stopping suddenly, she looked around and saw that the room was completely empty. She turned to go over to the back door, but at that moment she heard a faint gasping sound coming from somewhere behind the bar, so he hurried over and saw that the door to the cellar had been left open.

"Matt, are you down there?" she asked, walking over to the door and looking down the steps. The lights were off, so she figured he couldn't possibly be poking about among all the pipes and barrels. She turned to keep looking.

At the last second, however, she realized that the gasping sound was becoming more persistent, and that it definitely seemed to be coming from the cellar.

"Matt?"

Stepping through to the top of the steps, she took a moment to flick the light on, and then she began to carefully pick her way down.

The gasps continued.

"Matt, is that you?" she asked, as the steps creaked beneath her weight. "Matt, you should be careful down here, okay? Believe me, I know from experience just how easy it is to bash your head against one of those low beams, or to trip over, or to damn near get yourself killed down in this -"

Suddenly she spotted Matt sliding down against the far wall, dropping onto the floor as he reached up and grabbed his own throat.

"Matt?"

She rushed over and crouched next to him, and she immediately saw that his neck was red and sore, with scratch-marks in the skin. He seemed to be in a state of panic, and for a moment he tried to push her away, almost as if he thought she might be somebody else.

"Matt, what happened?" she asked. "What are you doing down here?"

She looked over her shoulder, but she saw nothing untoward in the room at all. When she turned back to Matt, however, she realized that he was still trying desperately to get his breath back.

"I saw her!" he gasped finally. "She was right here!"

"Who was?"

Looking around, frantic with fear, Matt tried to spot the woman. Realizing that she was nowhere to be seen, he tried to get to his feet, although he immediately struggled and he had to accept Sally's help as she hauled him up from the ground. Wincing as he felt a pain in his shoulder, he leaned against the wall for a moment to try to get his breath back.

"She was right here," he said finally, grabbing her arm and leading her to the steps. "She was trying to strangle me!"

"Who are you talking about?"

"Who do you think?" he snapped, turning to her. "Mildred Weaver, or whatever her name was. It had to have been her, right? It was this old woman, and she held my throat and she was asking where she could find someone named Annie Ashton. How can that not be her?"

Sally opened her mouth to reply, but for a moment she hesitated as she thought back to the little girl she'd seen upstairs, and to the message scratched into the wall.

"I saw something too," she said cautiously.

"A ghost?"

He waited for an answer, and then he

reached out and put a hand on the side of her arm.

"Sally," he said, barely able to get the words out, "did you see something too?"

Before she could say anything, however, the back door opened and Jane hurried inside, still smoking a cigarette.

"Hey, guys," Jane said, clearly trying to sound calmer than she felt as she headed to the table and grabbed her bag, "what's up? So, I was thinking that maybe it's time to shoot now. I don't want to stay up half the night, wasting time when I really should be asleep." She started sorting through her bag, although her hands were shaking violently. "This has been fun, we should do it again sometime."

"Are you okay?" Sally asked.

"I'm fine. Why do you ask?"

"You seem a little nervy there."

"Well, I said I'm fine," Jane added, as she slung her bag over her shoulder and began to make her way to the door. "Why do people always have to ask other people if they're fine? If someone's not fine and they want to talk about it, they'll talk about it, otherwise it's just another pointless question."

"Did something happen to you out in the garden?" Sally continued. "Jane, something really weird happened in here and -"

"Nothing happened in the garden!" Jane snapped, stopping and turning to her. "I didn't see anything, okay? So stop going on about it!"

"What did you see?" Matt asked.

"I just told you, I -"

"Because I think I saw Mildred Weaver," he added.

"And I think I saw Annie Ashton," Sally said. "You know... the little girl."

"No, neither of you saw anyone," Jane replied, no longer able to hide her sense of extreme agitation, "because they're long dead, you see? And the thing about dead people is that they stay dead, and you don't just find them wandering around in buildings, and they don't start talking to you or showing up in places. Don't you guys get it? This is just some immature game that makes you feel a little better about death. There's no such thing as ghosts!"

"You seem really rattled," Sally pointed out.

"Shut the hell up!"

"Jane, you're the one who wanted to do this in the first place," Sally continued. "You brought the board, you -"

"Screw the board!" Jane yelled, storming back to the table and grabbing the spirit board. "Do you know what I think about this homemade piece of crap? Really? Do you know my honest opinion about this whole sorry, miserable night that we've been enduring, and about this cheap, shoddy piece of garbage board made by one of Bradley's dumbass friends?"

With that, she slammed the board against the side of the table. When that failed to cause any damage, she bent it against her knee, and she was slowly able to tear it apart until finally she threw the two halves to the floor, where they landed near Sally's feet. And then, for good measure, Jane took one of the pieces and hurled it across the room, sending it bouncing off the far wall until it ricocheted off the bar and landed next to the cellar door.

"That's what I think about the stupid board!" Jane snarled, as she fumbled in her bag for more cigarettes. "You guys really need to learn when to recognize that something's a joke. It's kinda pathetic the way you bought into the idea of ghosts so easily, you're not -"

Before she could finish, the tape recorder fell from her bag and hit the floor.

"What's that doing here?" Sally asked, stepping closer. "It's running. Has it been going the whole time?"

"You don't get it," Jane muttered, crouching down and grabbing the recorder, quickly putting it back into her bag. "Damn it, this whole thing is a mess. At the start of the evening it all seemed so simple, I had a perfect plan and I knew exactly how to put it into action. Of course, real life always shows up and ruins things, doesn't it? If Kevin thinks he's getting his money back, though, he can sing for it. I did everything I promised, and I don't offer refunds."

"Kevin?" Sally said, shocked to hear that name, as Jane hurried to the door.

Sally turned to her.

"You mean Kevin, as in my ex-husband?"

Stopping at the door, Jane hesitated for a moment before slowly turning to her.

"You don't know my ex-husband," Sally continued. "You can't. I mean, it's impossible, he's never even been to Crowford."

"Yeah, well," Jane replied, "there's such a thing as telephones. And for your information, he's onto you, okay? He's got people crawling around, trying to nail you down, and..."

Her voice trailed off for a moment, and then she took a step back.

"Forget it," she added. "I don't need this drama in my life. Good luck, Sally. I hope you're really happy. I don't know how you possibly *can* be, not after what you did, but I don't want anything to do with this anymore. I've got enough craziness in my life already, without dealing with a bunch of other people who can't get their shit together." She paused. "Don't try to call me, okay? I was never your friend, not really, I only got close to you because someone paid me to, and I wouldn't expect you to ever forgive me for that. I'm sorry, but this is goodbye."

With that, she stormed out of the pub, letting the door slam shut behind her.

## CHAPTER FIFTEEN

"SO THAT WAS INTENSE," Matt said a couple of minutes later, as he set the two pieces of the broken spirit board on the table. "I don't know Jane very well, but I never had her down as someone who'd fly off the handle like that."

He headed over to the fireplace and tossed another log onto the dying flames.

"It's like she completely lost her mind," he added.

Barely listening to a word he was saying, Sally sat at the table and stared at the tape recorder. She'd switched it off, but she couldn't help thinking about the fact that it had been in Jane's bag the whole time. After arriving in Crowford, she'd struggled to make friends until Jane had shown up at the pub one night. They'd quickly become pretty close, but now Sally was starting to realize that the whole thing had been a sham.

Not only that, but her ex had been involved too.

"So what do you reckon spooked her so much?" Matt asked as he headed to the back door and looked out at the garden. He watched for a moment, before turning to Sally again. "We both saw something tonight, right? What do we do next? I mean, this is all pretty wacky, right? I don't know about you, but I didn't expect to see an actual ghost. Maybe a few hints of something, maybe something a little spooky, but I really didn't think I'd see a ghost just... standing there. And I definitely didn't think one would actually try to attack me."

He furrowed his brow for a moment.

"Is it possible that we imagined it all?" he asked. "Joint hallucinations are a thing, aren't they? What if we got ourselves all riled up so much, we conjured it up in our heads?"

He waited, but after a few seconds he realized that Sally was completely zoned out.

"Hey," he continued, stepping over to her and putting a hand on her shoulder, "if you -"

"He's not going to appear to me," she said suddenly, interrupting him.

"What do you mean?"

"My son," she added, still staring at the tape recorder. "I've been fooling myself this whole time, but the truth is, he's never going to let me see him again. Not after..."

Her voice trailed off.

For a moment, in her mind's eye, she thought back to the night she and Tommy had arrived in Crowford. She'd gone down to fetch some more items from the car, and when she'd returned she'd found Tommy writhing in agony on the bed. As tears filled her eyes, she remembered how he'd begged her to end the pain, and how she'd tried giving him the usual medication. Something about the long journey had seemed to wear him down more than usual, and even the pills had done nothing to help. He'd begun to shake violently, and he'd coughed up so much blood.

"Mummy, please," she remembered him crying, "I don't want it to hurt anymore!"

"Everything's going to be fine," she'd replied. "Trust me, sweetheart. Mummy's right here with you. Mummy's not going anywhere."

"I want it to stop!" he'd sobbed, clutching his belly. "Why won't it stop?"

"Sally?" Matt said cautiously, taking a seat opposite her. "We should probably think about calling this a night. I don't know about you, but I've seen enough to give me some pretty harsh nightmares, and if there's a chance that there are some actual ghosts here, then -"

"I killed him," she whispered.

"I'm sorry?"

A tear ran down her cheek, followed by another.

"I brought him to Crowford because I knew he was going to die," she explained, "but I thought he had a few more weeks at least. Then, on the night we arrived, he was in so much pain, he said it was like his insides were burning. The doctors had warned me that it'd get like that, and that the medication would only do so much. I sat there and I looked at him and I realized that the rest of his short little life was going to be nothing but suffering and agony. And I couldn't bear that."

"I don't..."

Matt's voice trailed off as he began to understand what she meant.

"I don't know why the coroner didn't say anything," she continued. "Maybe he didn't catch it, or maybe he did but he didn't want to believe it, or maybe he thought that I did the right thing, but..." She finally managed to look Matt in the eye. "You've never had kids, so you can't possibly imagine what it's like to see your own son dying in agony right in front of you."

"No," he replied, "I suppose I can't."

"He had a month left at the absolute maximum," she told him. "More likely it would have been a couple of weeks. And they would have been hell for him. No mother could watch their son go through something like that. In some way, I think as soon as I took him away from the hospital, I knew how it was going to have to end. So I took the..."

For a moment, she couldn't get the words out.

"Sally," Matt said after a moment, "maybe -"

"I took the pillow," she said, as her voice trembled with sorrow, "and I tried to make it as quick and painless as possible."

They sat in silence for a moment, as Sally thought back to that awful moment, and as Matt finally realized the truth about Tommy's death.

"I don't know how Kevin came to suspect it," she continued. "I guess he just figured that I'm that kind of person. I murdered my own son."

"No," Matt replied, reaching over and taking hold of her hands, "you didn't murder him. You wanted to make sure that he didn't suffer anymore, you wanted to protect him."

"Do you really believe that?" she asked through gritted teeth. "Would you have done the same thing if it had been your child?"

"I don't know what -"

"Would you?" she snapped. "Tell me honestly, would you have done what I did?"

Matt considered the question for a moment.

"No," he said finally, pulling his hands back

across the table. "No, I don't think I would. I mean, I don't think I could, but that doesn't mean that you're wrong. Maybe it just takes extra strength to be able to step up and..."

Again, his voice trailed off.

"There's nothing left," Sally continued. "I've tried over and over again to tell myself that I did the merciful thing, but deep down I know that I'm a monster. I brought Tommy to Crowford because I wanted a chance to have his ghost around, and then I did something that guarantees he won't ever want to see me again. Even if his ghost happened to be here, there's no way he'd be willing to talk to me or to listen to me. He must hate me."

Matt tried to think of something to say that might make her feel better, but he found that he was unable to come up with any words. He felt hopelessly out of his depth, as if he couldn't even begin to imagine what it must have been like for Sally as she watched her son die.

"It's okay," Sally said, "I get it. You're shocked. And you don't have to worry about wondering whether or not to tell anyone, because I think it's time I did that myself. I've been a coward. I just need to go to the police and tell them everything. I have absolutely no idea what'll happen to me, but I'll take it. And do you know the worst thing?"

She paused.

"I'd do it again," she added. "God forbid, but if I was in that situation again, watching my poor boy die in such extreme agony, I'd do whatever it took to end his suffering as quickly as possible."

Reaching up, she wiped away another tear.

"Okay," she said, "I think that's probably enough of that for one night. Why don't we try to -"

Suddenly a loud thud rang out, banging against the floor of the room directly above the bar area. Sally and Matt both looked up, just as they heard a second, even louder thud that caused the ceiling to shudder slightly.

"What the hell's going on up there?" Matt asked.

"I don't know," Sally replied, "but -"

Suddenly they both heard a scream, and Sally immediately got to her feet.

"It's her," she stammered, thinking back to the little girl she'd seen earlier. "That's Alice!"

As that name let her lips, they both heard another thud, this time as something or someone slammed a door upstairs. Sally turned and looked at Matt, and then she raced through to the hallway.

"Where are you going?" Matt called out, before getting up and hurrying after her. "Sally, wait!"

# CHAPTER SIXTEEN

"ANNIE?" SALLY CALLED OUT as soon as she reached the top of the stairs, just as the banging sounds stopped. "Annie, where are you?"

She waited, and a moment later she heard Matt hurrying up after her.

"What the hell's going on?" he asked, before spotting the scratched message on the wall. "Wait, was that always there?"

"It appeared earlier, while I was up here," she said cautiously, turning and looking at the various doors, waiting for even the slightest hint of the little girl's location. "She's terrified of someone finding her, and I don't think it takes much to figure out who."

"And we're talking about ghosts, right?"

She turned to him.

"I just wanted to make sure that we're on the same page," he added, looking a little pale as he began to realize the truth. "I guess messing with that spirit board really opened up a can of worms, huh? Do you think maybe the smart move would be to go back downstairs and, I don't know, get out of here?"

Before she could finish, Sally realized someone was sobbing in one of the bedrooms. Heading over to the door that led into Jerry's room, she stopped just as the sobs came to an abrupt halt.

"In here," she said, with fear in her voice. "She's in here."

Matt looked over his shoulder, back down the stairs, before making his way over to join her.

"I don't mean to pull rank," he said, "but I'm pretty sure I met Mrs. Weaver down in the cellar, and she didn't seem to be in a very good mood. I'd really rather not meet her again."

"Did she mention Annie at all?"

"She asked me where she's been hiding."

Sally turned to him.

"This doesn't make a whole lot of sense," he continued. "Mildred Weaver died more than half a century ago, right? And I think it's fair to say that little Annie must have died around that time too. Are you really suggesting that they've been engaged in some ghostly game of hide-and-seek ever since?"

"I'm not suggesting anything," she replied, before turning to look into the room again as the sobbing sound returned. "I'm just seeing what I'm seeing, and hearing what I'm hearing."

"And Tommy -"

"This isn't about Tommy right now," she added, interrupting him. "This is about Annie."

She stepped into the room and looked around. Although the sobs continued, she realized that it was difficult to pin them down to an exact spot. As she made her way around the bed, however, she began to feel as if the little girl might be hiding under the desk that stood over by the window.

"Hey, Annie," she said, hoping to keep from scaring the girl. "Annie Ashton, right? Is that your name?"

"If she's here," Matt said, "then why have we only just noticed?"

"It's like you pointed out," Sally replied. "We messed with the spirit board. Either we brought the ghosts here, or they were always here and we just never saw them until now."

Reaching the desk, she crouched down and looked at the small space beyond the chair. There was just enough room for a child to fit, and Sally couldn't help imagining a poor, sobbing girl curled up tight into a ball, desperately trying to keep from being seen.

"Annie?" she whispered. "I saw you earlier. I mean, I think I did. Can I see you again? Is that allowed?"

As he watched Sally, Matt suddenly became aware of a sound coming from somewhere nearby. He stepped back out onto the landing and looked down the stairs, just as one of the boards near the bottom let out a slow, distinctive creak.

"Uh, Sally?" he said cautiously. "I don't mean to worry you, but I think there's a slight chance that someone's coming up to join us. And whoever they are, I can't exactly *see* them."

He waited for her to reply, but she was busy trying to coax Annie out of hiding.

"Sally?" he called out, as he heard a creaking sound coming from another, higher step, "I've got a really bad feeling about this. I hate to rush you, but I think Mrs. Weaver might be on her way."

Another board groaned, and this time the banister shook slightly, as if a dead, unseen hand was gripping its side as a figure slowly made its way up toward the pub's top floor.

Instinctively, Matt took a step back.

"Sally, I really think we need to do something about this," he continued, watching the empty staircase but convinced that a figure remained just out of sight. Remembering the terrifying sensation of having a dead hand on his throat, he took another step back. "Sally, I'm not joking, someone's coming! I can hear -"

Before he was able to finish, he felt a rush of cold air reach the top of the stairs. Taking yet another step back, he flinched as he waited for the woman to appear again; instead, he felt the cold air move past, brushing against him as if an invisible figure was making its way over to the door.

"Sally, she's coming your way! I don't know what to do!"

"Annie," Sally said, still crouching next to the desk, desperately trying to stay as calm as possible, "I need -"

Behind her, the door bumped against the wall, as if it had just been knocked by someone. Sally looked over for a moment, before turning back to the desk.

"Annie, I get that you're scared," she continued, "and I really don't blame you right now, okay? To tell the truth, I'm kinda scared too and -"

Suddenly the chair scraped to one side, almost hitting her in the face, as Sally heard a bumping sound. She turned and listened as the sound scrambled away and around to the far side of the bed, almost as if the little girl was trying to find somewhere else to hide.

"Annie?" she said cautiously. "What -"

In that moment, she felt a patch of cold air brush against her face. She looked up, but she saw no sign of anyone, even as she realized that a figure was slowly walking past. Although she wanted to call out, for a few seconds Sally was completely frozen by fear, convinced that at any moment she'd spot the ghostly figure of Mildred Weaver.

"What's happening in there?" Matt asked, stopping in the doorway. "Sally, where is she?"

"She's under the bed," she replied, listening to the continued sobbing sound. "I don't know exactly what's happening, but I think -"

The girl screamed again, just as something bumped against the bed's other side.

"Leave her alone!" Sally called out, before she could stop herself. She looked up at the spot where she assumed Mildred Weaver must be standing. "Do you hear me?" she continued, not really knowing what else she could try. "Leave her alone and -"

Suddenly a book flew off the nightstand and slammed into the side of Sally's face. Letting out a pained gasp, she turned away as the book fell to the floor; when she reached up and touched the side of her face, she realized that the book had hit her with enough force to cut her cheek.

"Get out of there!" Matt hissed. "Sally, I'm serious, you don't know what she's capable of! She almost strangled me!"

"We can't leave the girl in here," she replied, leaning down and looking under the bed, but seeing nothing except a few of Jerry's storage boxes. "Annie, if -"

The bed shuddered again, as if once more it had been hit by an invisible force. Although she was still trying desperately to spot Annie, Sally was starting to realize that the little girl was somehow just beyond the limits of her perception. She knew she had to try to keep her safe, but a moment later the bed shuddered again, this time moving a couple of inches.

Hearing a scrambling sound, Sally realized that Annie was clambering out from under the bed's other side, and then she watched as Matt stepped out of the way.

"Someone just ran past me!" he gasped. "I swear, I just felt someone run right past me and go out onto the landing!"

"She's trying to get away from Mildred Weaver," Sally replied, before feeling another rush of cold air as something moved back across the room. "I don't know why, but it's as if Mildred won't give up until she's got her!"

"Another one just went past me!" Matt shouted, trying not to panic as he stumbled into the room and then turned to look back out toward the landing. "That one was much bigger!"

"The ghost of Mildred Weaver is chasing the ghost of Annie Ashton," Sally pointed out, as they both heard the sound of another door slamming open nearby. "And I don't think she's going to stop until she's caught her!"

# CHAPTER SEVENTEEN

"JANE? HEY, WHAT ARE you making so much noise for?"

Stopping at the bottom of the stairs, Bradley looked through to the kitchen and saw that Jane was sitting at the table with her head in her hands. He'd heard her getting home a few minutes earlier, and since then she'd been slamming things around with such force that he'd eventually had to make his way down to check on her. Now, as he wandered over to the doorway, he realized he could hear her sobbing.

"Are you okay?" he asked.

"Do I look okay?" she snapped, keeping her hands over her face. "Seriously, Bradley, do you just ask stupid questions all the time? Sometimes, if you can tell that someone's not okay, it's fine to just leave them alone and not bother them. That might actually be what they want. Do you have *any* understanding of how to interact with other people at all?"

"Did something happen to you?"

Finally she looked at him, and he was shocked to see that tears had left trails of black make-up down her face.

"I didn't get attacked, if that's what you mean," she said through gritted teeth. "I just had a really shitty night, and I thought I'd fix myself something to eat, but apparently someone decided to take all my stuff from the fridge. Seriously, does nobody in this house have any respect for anyone else's property?"

"It's three in the morning," he pointed out. "Where have you been until three in the goddamn morning?"

"That's really none of your business."

"But..."

His voice trailed off for a moment as he remembered his earlier encounter with Jane, up in his room.

"Did you try out my friend's spirit board?" he asked.

"Yes, Bradley," she replied, "we tried out the spirit board. We had a great old time with the stupid thing. Are you happy now?"

"What happened?"

She stared at him for a moment, before

sighing as she got to her feet.

"Nothing happened, you moron," she told him as she pushed past him and headed to the stairs. "It's just a stupid board. Oh, and by the way, I'm sorry but I didn't bring it back. It got broken. If you have an issue with that, I'm sorry, but it's not like you were looking after it, anyway. I actually did you a favor by helping get some of the garbage out of your room." She began to make her way upstairs. "You can thank me another time."

"Whatever," he replied. "As long as you ended the session properly."

Stopping, she hesitated for a moment, before leaning over the railing and looking down at him.

"What are you on about now?" she asked cautiously.

"You knew to end the session properly, didn't you?" he continued. "You have to say goodbye to the ghost properly."

"Or what?"

"Or... I don't know, but I've always heard that really bad things can happen. The spirits are... I'm not sure, but it's like the session stays open, and that's when horror movie stuff starts going on." He paused. "Did you end the session properly and say goodbye to any spirits you'd contacted, Jane? Did you move the marker onto the spot with the word Farewell?"

"I thought you didn't know how it worked?"

"I don't, but... I mean, that part's just obvious."

He waited for her to reply.

"Of course we finished it properly," she replied after a pause. "We're not complete idiots, you know. Not like you."

"Okay, that's a relief," he said as she stormed up to her room. "I'd hate to think that you left it open, because that's when things can get really freaky."

\*\*\*

"Idiot!" she muttered under her breath as she leaned back against her bedroom door, letting it slam shut. "Suddenly he thinks he's some kind of expert on ghosts, huh? I'm sure he is, from the comfort of his mess of a bedroom, surrounded by all those stupid books."

She took a deep breath and tried to pull herself together, but deep down she could still feel a rumbling sense of panic. Ever since she'd stormed out of the pub, she'd been unable to shake the feeling that something was wrong; she couldn't put her finger on exactly what was causing her to feel that way, but on the way home she'd almost felt as if she was being pursued. She'd checked over her shoulder a few times as she'd made her way through the dark streets of Crowford, and she hadn't spotted anyone. Nevertheless, she'd been extremely relieved to get home, and she was disappointed to find that the strange sensation was still with her.

She looked around her room, but of course there was no sign of anyone.

As she heard Bradley's footsteps stomping up the stairs, she realized she could suddenly smell petrol. The stench quickly became overpowering, to the point that she finally pulled the door open and stepped back out onto the landing, just as Bradley was about to head into his own room. Putting her sleeve against her nose, Jane tried to keep from gagging.

"Are you okay?" Bradley asked.

"What are you doing?" she replied. "The house reeks!"

He stared at her, not understanding what she meant.

"Have you got petrol in here?" she continued. "Is it one of the others?"

"I've got no idea what you're talking about," he told her. "Jane, are you high on something?"

"Are you telling me you can't smell that?"

He looked around.

"Forget it," she said with a sigh, heading back into her room and shutting the door again, before hurrying to the window and sliding it open. Leaning out, she took a few deep breaths, and then she pulled back into the room and waited for the foul smell to dissipate.

A moment later, however, she realized she could feel something between her fingers. Looking down, she was surprised to see small black particles of grit on her hands. She tried to wipe them off, but more seemed to be appearing as if from nowhere and after a few seconds she realized that the smell of petrol was getting stronger. Then, as she turned to look back across the room, she winced as she felt a sudden pain on her left cheek.

Reaching up, she was surprised to feel something poking out from the skin. She rushed over to the mirror in the corner and took a look, and she saw that a thin sliver of glass had somehow become embedded in her face.

"What the..."

She began to slide the glass out, and she grimaced as she saw that it was smeared with blood.

"Okay," she whispered, "I'm losing my mind here. Did I fall over on the way home and forget? I didn't have *that* many drinks at the pub."

Once the piece of glass was out, she set it down on the shelf, and then she stared at her own reflection. She told herself to stay calm, but after a few seconds she began to realize that another pain was throbbing in her side, somewhere down near the bottom of the ribs on her left side. She hesitated, before slowly lifting her shirt up until she saw that one side of her chest was badly bruised, with discolored purplish-yellow skin spreading almost all the way up to her armpit. Horrified, she touched one of the darker sections of the bruise, and she let out a gasp as she felt a burning pain.

Thinking back to her journey home, she knew for certain that she'd suffered no accidents. Yet as the smell of petrol lingered, and as she looked down at her left hand and saw that the palm was badly grazed, she was starting to realize that these spontaneous wounds seemed strangely familiar.

Not from that night, but from a night several years earlier.

"No," she whispered, just as she heard a rasping sound coming from over her shoulder.

Not daring to turn and look, she stared at the mirror and told herself that she was imagining things. After just a few seconds, however, she realized that she could see else something reflected in the glass, something that appeared to be over on the far side of the room, watching her from the shadows.

"No!" she said firmly, clenching her fists, determined to not see the face that even now was emerging from the darkness. "This is impossible! You're not here!"

She heard the sound of bones creaking; dry, old bones that hadn't moved in a long time. She flinched, and then finally she turned to prove to herself that she was wrong, only to find herself face to face with the one face she'd hoped to never see again, which was also the one face that was burned indelibly in her mind.

"Why did you make me walk?" her dead sister Olivia asked, barely able to get the words out as her broken jaw clicked with every movement. "Why did you let me die?"

## CHAPTER EIGHTEEN

"I THINK SHE CAME down here," Sally said, stepping through into the bar area and then stopping again to listen. "I'm sure I heard someone on the stairs."

"I didn't hear anything," Matt replied, stopping right behind her and looking out across the empty room. "I haven't heard anything since we left the room upstairs. Are they like some kind of ghostly Tom and Jerry?"

"Quiet!" she said, taking a couple of steps forward, looking around for any hint of movement.

Matt waited, but he was becoming increasingly convinced that they were on a hiding to nothing. For one thing, he'd heard none of the little bumps and knocking sounds that Sally claimed had led her downstairs; for another, he was far from convinced that – even if the ghosts were real – anything could be done to help them.

Still, they stood in silence for a few more seconds, each of them waiting for even the faintest sign that the little girl might be nearby. The pub remained eerily quiet; so quiet, in fact, that Matt began to wonder whether the hush was actually some kind of presence, as if the ghost of Mildred Weaver had somehow shut the rest of the world out and sealed the pub off in its own strange realm. Although he desperately wanted to get to the door, however, Matt knew that first he had to help Sally end whatever they'd started.

"We need to finish this," he said finally. "Quickly."

"What do you mean?" Sally asked, turning to him.

"You must have seen it in movies. That spirit board has the word Farewell on it, so we tape it back together and we say goodbye to the spirit. To Mildred Weaver, or to Annie Ashton, or to both of them. It's the only sensible option."

"We can't leave that poor little girl to get chased around!"

"Yes, we can!" he said firmly, stepping over to her. "Think about it for a moment, Sally. Before we made contact with them, before we even knew they were here, they must have been up to this for decades. And Mildred has never managed to catch

Annie, so why would she catch her now? In fact, what if we've actually made things worse by somehow making the ghosts more visible? The best thing to do, to help Annie, might be to get this over with."

He waited for a reply, but she seemed unconvinced.

"What would you even do if you found them?" he continued. "Do you actually have a plan?"

"No," she replied, "but -"

"Then the smart thing is to end the session. Let's do it right now!"

"But the board -"

"Do you have any tape?" he asked, heading over to the two pieces of the broken board and sliding them back together. "Hurry."

Running behind the bar, Sally grabbed a roll of tape and then made her way over to join him.

"There are only two of us," she pointed out as she handed him the tape. "Didn't we establish earlier that we need three in order to contact a spirit?"

"We've already contacted her," he said, "that's not the problem." He began to tape the board back together. "I don't know all the rules, Sally, but it might be possible to end this with just the two of us. And I don't know about you, but right now I'm willing to try just about anything. Unless you think it's worth trying to get Jane back, which I'm pretty sure isn't what anyone wants right now."

"What about Annie?"

"She was fine before we did this. I really think we might be the ones who are putting her in danger."

Sally watched as he carefully taped the board together, and then – realizing that the marker was missing – she began to look around. Spotting it in the corner, she hurried over and grabbed it before heading back to the table. As she and Matt sat down, however, she couldn't help looking around once again, just in case there was any sign of Mildred or Annie.

"We didn't check the cellar," she pointed out.

"There's no time for -"

"I'm going to look!"

Getting to her feet, she hurried around behind the bar.

"You're dragging this out!" he called after her, unable to hide the desperation in his voice. "Sally, you can't do anything to save her! All you can do is help me to put this all right!"

He waited, and then he sighed as he heard her heading down the stairs. Telling himself that there was no need to panic just yet, he took a moment to continue fixing the board, and then – realizing that he could do with another drink – he got to his feet. He headed over to the fireplace first and threw on a few more logs, and then he made his way behind the bar and poured himself a drink.

"No-one ever listens to me," he muttered. "Isn't it just possible, for once, that I might have a good idea?"

Glancing across the room, he watched once again in case a ghostly figure might materialize. He tried to remind himself that ghosts weren't supposed to be real, although the cold hand on his throat had certainly felt real in the basement. Reaching up, he touched the side of his neck and felt the scratches, and then he glanced over his shoulder.

"Found anything?" he called out.

"Not yet!" Sally shouted from the cellar. "I'm just going to keep looking for a moment. If she's hiding, it might not be obvious where to find her."

"Yeah, sure," he said as he finished pouring the pint. He took a sip, and then he carried it back over to the table. "We've messed with something we should have left well enough alone and -"

Suddenly catching his own reflection in the back door, he froze as soon as he saw that Mildred Weaver was standing right behind him. Spinning around, almost spilling his beer, he found that she was gone. He turned to look at the door again, and this time the horrifying figure was nowhere to be seen.

"Okay, I'm pretty sure she's not down there," Sally said as she hurried up the stairs. "To be honest, though, I'm really not sure. If she's hiding, and if she's got lots of practice at keeping herself out of sight, then I don't know whether we'd ever be able to find her."

She made her way to the table and turned to Matt, and then she hesitated for a moment as she realized that he seemed shocked by something.

"What happened?" she asked.

He stared at the door for a few seconds, before taking his seat again.

"Let's just get on with this," he said, taking the marker and placing it on the board. "Sally, are you going to stand there, or are you going to help me? If we can close the session, this'll all be over."

Sitting opposite him, she reached out and touched the marker with the tip of a finger.

"I just want you to know that I'm sorry I dragged you into this," she told him. "I -"

"Spirit!" he called out, interrupting her. "I know you're here. I know you're close. We're here now to tell you that we're leaving. We won't be communicating with you anymore, so we're saying goodbye."

He waited.

"Now what?" Sally asked.

"Farewell," he said again, and then he pushed the marker over to the corresponding word on the board. "Don't worry," he told Sally, "I did that on purpose."

"Okay," she replied, "but -"

Before she could finish, the marker raced back across the board until it reached the word No, where it stopped.

"I didn't do *that*," Matt said.

"Me neither."

"We're leaving now," he announced, more firmly than before. "It's not negotiable. We're saying goodbye to you."

He forced the marker back over to the word Farewell, but it immediately shot back to No.

"I don't think she likes the idea," Sally suggested. "Do you think it's because there are only two of us?"

"She doesn't have to like it," he replied, before taking a deep breath and preparing to try again. "There are two of us, and there's only one of her, so this conversation is over, regardless of what she thinks." He hesitated. "We're leaving now," he said firmly. "You can go back to whatever your existence was like before we disturbed you. That's the final word. Farewell."

With that, he and Sally moved the marker back to Farewell.

They waited.

"Did it work?" Sally asked after a few seconds had passed. She looked around. "Did -"

Suddenly the marker slid back to No, and then it flew off the board and hit Sally in the face before spinning away and hitting the wall. Letting out a pained gasp, Sally turned away; when she turned back to Matt, blood was running from a cut on her chin.

"Call me crazy," she said, her voice trembling with fear, "but I don't think she's willing to let this end just yet."

# CHAPTER NINETEEN

"LEAVE ME ALONE!" JANE screamed, stumbling out of her room and then tripping, falling across the landing and hitting the wall before sliding down to the floor.

Staring up at the open door opposite, she held her breath as she waited to see her sister's dead face again. The prospect filled her with terror, but at the same time she couldn't look away. A moment later, however, she heard another door opening, and she finally turned to see that Bradley was emerging from his room.

"Are you for real?" he asked. "Are you tripping, Jane? I heard you ranting and raving in your room, what the hell was that all about?"

"I..."

She hesitated, before looking at the door

again.

"Go and see," she told him.

"What?"

"Go and look in my room," she continued, as her voice trembled with fear, "and tell me what you see."

Bradley hesitated, before making his way to the door and looking through into her bedroom.

"I see the room of a skanky bitch who criticizes other people when her own place isn't exactly the cleanest in the world."

"Do you see anyone?" she shouted, momentarily losing control. She felt as if the entire world was collapsing all around her. "Do you see my sister?"

He turned to her.

"Your sister?" he said cautiously. "Didn't your sister die in an accident a few years ago?"

"Do you see her?" she asked through gritted teeth. "Yes or no?"

"No," he told her, "I don't see her. What's all this about? Do I need to call an ambulance so you can go to the hospital and get your stomach pumped?"

"She was there," she replied, slowly getting to her feet, not daring to take her gaze away from the door. "I could see her. I could hear her. I could smell her. It's almost as if I was starting to *become* her. It was like I was getting all the injuries she suffered when she was hit by that..."

Her voice trailed off. For a moment, she could only think back to the night when she'd told Olivia to get lost, when she'd made her walk home instead of giving her the ride she'd promised. That had been the last time she'd ever seen her alive. After that night, Jane's world had come crashing down, and she'd never quite recovered. She'd always been able to push the worst of it out of her mind, but now something seemed to have changed.

"Okay, I think you're having some kind of breakdown," Bradley told her. "Let's call a truce for tonight, okay? I want to help you, and you're really freaking me out."

"She said she blamed me," she replied, as she felt a knot of fear starting to tighten in her chest. "She said it was all my fault." She slowly turned to him. "I think she's come back to make me pay."

***

Racing out of the house, Jane stumbled and bumped against a parked car, and then she set off along the pavement. She heard Bradley calling after her, but she told herself that she had no more time to stop and talk. All she wanted was to get as far away as possible from her dead sister. She told herself that she hadn't really seen Olivia, that the evening's strange events had simply messed with her head, but still...

She had to run.

Reaching the end of the street, however, she realized that she didn't know where to go. Unable to simply stand still, she began to follow the road to the right, heading up the gentle rise that led to the train bridge. Traffic lights blinked in the distance, organizing empty road, as Jane made her way over the bridge. She glanced down at the train tracks far below, and at the station a little further off, and then she headed down the other side until she reached the crossroads with *The Brew House* on one corner.

She looked around, and then she let out a shocked gasp as she saw a figure standing over by one of the crossings.

"No," she whispered, even though she could already tell that the figure was staring straight at her, "it's not you."

She forced herself to turn and keep going, past a row of shops and then over to the edge of the supermarket parking lot. Telling herself that the other figure had simply been some other poor soul who'd been out for a wander at damn near three in the morning, she managed to keep from looking over her shoulder, and she felt some degree of calm as she realized that she couldn't hear footsteps following her along the street. Finally, as she reached the turn-off for the supermarket, she stopped and took a deep breath, and she told herself that it would be safe to look.

She slowly turned, and to her immense relief there was no sign of anyone.

"Told you," she said out loud. "It was nothing but a load of crap that got into my head."

Still, she looked around for a moment longer, before deciding to take the road that led into town. She figured that she could call on one of her friends and hang out for a few hours; Beth would usually be up all night, and so would Carrie or Liam. As she shuffled past another row of dark shops, however, she once again began to feel as if she was being watched. No matter how hard she tried to ignore that sensation, she felt it getting stronger and stronger, until finally she stopped as she looked ahead and saw the High Street in the distance. Somehow she knew that something was waiting for her there, so she turned and doubled back on herself, before picking a new direction and making her way along the next street.

"There's no-one there," she whispered, "there's no -"

"Jane."

Startled, she spun around.

No-one was behind her, but her dead sister's voice had seemed so clear for a moment.

"Go away!" she spluttered before she had a chance to stop herself. "I know you're not real, so just leave me alone!"

She waited, but a moment later she saw the lights of a car approaching a nearby junction. She instinctively pulled back out of sight around the corner, and then she watched as a police car slowly drove past. Although she was doing nothing wrong, she knew the police would have stopped to ask her if she was okay, and she had no idea how to even begin to explain why she was out. Instead, she waited until the car had disappeared into the distance, and then she set off again, this time with a specific destination in mind.

Lofty.

She was going to visit Lofty.

He'd be awake; if he wasn't, she'd knock on his door until he had no choice.

She picked up the pace a little, resisting the urge to run. Again, she was troubled by the sense that she was being watched or followed, and she was finding it harder and harder to put that feeling out of her mind. After a few seconds she broke into a jog, but then she stopped at the next corner as she realized she was getting close to *The Crowford Hoy*. She felt certain that Sally and Matt would have long since packed up and abandoned their stupid game, but she still didn't much fancy the idea of accidentally bumping into either of them, so she picked a slightly longer route to Lofty's house, one that took her along Fentinel Street.

Glancing over her shoulder, she checked

once again that there was no sign of anyone, and then she took the next left.

"Why did you let me die?" Olivia asked, suddenly standing right in front of her, her body bearing all the injuries she'd sustained four years ago. Tears were streaming down her cheeks. "Why didn't you pick me up like you promised?"

Jane stared at her for a moment, struck by the horrific sight of her little sister's corpse, and then she turned and ran. Racing back along Orange Street, all she knew was that she had to get as far away as possible, and – as she rushed across the next junction – she barely even noticed a flash of light to her right.

In an instant, a van slammed into her side, shattering her ribs and sending her flying through the air until she hit a lamppost. Unable to even scream, she spun around and hit the tarmac with enough speed that her body scraped along the ground for several meters before coming to a rest in the gutter.

As one final gurgle rose from her throat, Jane looked up and saw the church spire nearby, and she realized that she was at the exact same junction where her sister had died after being hit by a car. She tried to move, to run, to cry out, but her body was broken. A strong smell of spilled petrol filled her nostrils, and she could feel gravel and dirt against her hands as she made one last attempt to sit up. Someone was shouting nearby, trying to raise the alarm as footsteps hurried closer, but Jane could only blink as her life drained away. By the time the van's driver reached her, she was dead.

# CHAPTER TWENTY

"IT'S LIKE WE'VE OPENED a door to something," Matt said, sitting at the table and staring down at the taped-together spirit board, "and now we can't close it. She won't let us."

He hesitated, before sliding the board closer and examining the torn section.

"What if we've missed a piece that got damaged?" he asked. "You know what it's like in horror films, ghosts are always real sticklers for the rules. Some of them can be really pedantic at times. What if a tiny piece is missing and that's why we weren't able to say goodbye?"

He turned the board over, but he could see no gaps.

"Matt?"

"I guess maybe it's because there were only

two of us," he added. "That must be it after all. It's really obvious, you even said it yourself. It takes three people to get anything done with that thing. It won't work with just the two of us."

"Matt?"

"All we managed to do was annoy her. Right now, we have no way to force Mildred Weaver to listen to us, or to make her do anything we want. Why is she even after that little girl, anyway? It's like she's obsessed."

"Matt?"

"What?"

He continued to examine the board, but for a moment Sally said nothing.

"You haven't looked at me," she managed finally.

He turned to her.

"That's the first time you've looked at me since I told you," she continued. "Properly, I mean. Since I told you what I did to Tommy."

"Nonsense," he replied. "I looked at you a load of times."

"I can see it in your eyes. You think I'm a terrible person."

"This isn't the time to talk about any of that," he told her. "In case you forgot, we've got a situation here."

"There's been no sign of Annie or Mildred Weaver since we tried to say goodbye," Sally pointed out. "Matt, I know what you must think of me. Believe me, I think the same thing. I killed my son. It doesn't matter that I thought I was doing it for the right reasons, it doesn't matter that I ended his suffering. I know exactly what I did, and I know that I can never be forgiven." She paused. "I'm definitely going to confess. First thing in the morning. Whatever happens, happens, but I can't live like this."

"You did what you had to do," he replied, looking back down at the board. He knew that Sally was right, that looking at her made him feel uncomfortable; he wanted to prove her wrong, but he didn't quite have the strength.

"You still can't quite look me in the eye for long," she pointed out. "It's okay. I get it."

He stared at the board, before turning to her. And then, before he could say another word, he saw a flashing blue light pass the pub, and he realized he could hear voices in the distance.

"Is something happening out there?" he asked, getting to his feet and hurrying to the window.

He pulled the blind aside and peered out, and sure enough he could see more lights in the distance.

"I think there's been an accident," he said, turning to Sally. "I can see an ambulance. I think someone might be hurt."

***

"What happened?" he asked a couple of minutes later, as he and Sally reached the corner of Orange Street and saw a van parked in the middle of the road. A little further off, an ambulance crew had begun to tend to a body on the ground, while two police cars were parked nearby.

"A girl got hit by a car," a woman explained, wearing a dressing gown. "I was already awake, I was having trouble sleeping, and I heard it all. The driver's over there. He says she ran out into the middle of the road before he had a chance to touch the brakes."

"This is the same spot where Jane's sister died," Sally whispered.

Matt turned to her.

"It was before I came to Crowford," she continued. "You must remember it, right?"

"Vaguely," he admitted. "Didn't she get hit by a car while she was walking home?"

"Jane always blamed herself," Sally said, as she felt a growing sense of unease in the pit of her stomach. "When she was drunk, at least. That was pretty much the only time she was ever willing to talk about it. She was supposed to give her sister a lift home from some class, but she blew her off to go out with some guy instead. The girl walked home and got hit by a car along the way. Jane's parents never forgave her, I don't think they even spoke to her again."

"I remember that too," the woman said, with a deflated tone to her voice. "I'm telling you, if it happens a third time round here, I might think about moving. Then again, this junction's going to start getting a bad reputation soon, I might have to get started before everyone else comes up with the same idea." She sniffed in the cold night air. "Something like this never has a good impact on property prices."

"Wait," Sally said, spotting a bag on the ground near one of the lampposts, "is that..."

She hesitated, before making her way around the side of the small crowd and heading to the post. Crouching down, she picked up the scuffed bag and saw immediately that she'd been right: it was Jane's bag, but she was pretty sure that Jane had gone the other way after leaving the pub earlier.

Turning, she looked over at the body on the ground. Just as one of the paramedics moved a sheet over the body, she saw the side of Jane's face.

"No!" she shouted, starting to rush over, only for a police officer to step in the way and stop her.

"I can't let you go over there," he said firmly.

"That's my friend!"

She tried to break free of the officer's grip, but he was holding her too firmly.

"Is she okay?" she asked. "Please, tell me she's okay!"

"I'm sorry," the officer replied, "there's nothing we can do for her now. We need to notify her next of kin."

"She can't be dead!" Sally sobbed. "There's got to be some kind of mistake!"

"This is the bag that was on the ground, isn't it?" the officer asked, as Sally stepped back. He reached out and took the bag from her trembling hands. "I'm going to have to ask you to move back, unless you have any information about how she came to be out here tonight."

Too horrified to even hear what the man was saying, Sally could only stare in horror at the shape on the ground. She told herself that it couldn't be true, but at the same time she'd seen Jane's face for herself. Even from the body language of the paramedics, she could already see that there was no sense of urgency, nothing to indicate that they thought anything could be done to save the woman on the ground.

"Come on, let's get you out of here," Matt said, trying to steer her away.

"Do you know what she was doing before she ran into the road?" the officer asked Sally. "It's rather late for a young woman to be out and about, especially on her own. Were you with her?"

"No, she wasn't," Matt explained. "We were inside, we just heard the commotion."

"Then you really need to stay back and let us do our job," the officer told him. "The bag might be evidence, you really shouldn't have picked it up. Please, there's nothing you can do."

"She knows," Matt replied, leading Sally away. "She's sorry."

Reaching a bench near the church railings, Matt helped her sit down.

"Why did I let her leave?" she sobbed, putting her hands over her face. "I knew she was upset, I could see something was wrong, but I was so angry that she'd been talking to Kevin. I still shouldn't have let her go, though. I should have made her stay and talk to me!"

"That was an hour ago, or more," he pointed out. "She obviously didn't just run out here and get hurt."

He looked over toward the ambulance for a moment.

"This isn't your fault, Sally," he continued, as he saw the body on the ground, covered by a dark sheet. "Whatever happened..."

His voice trailed off.

"This is exactly where her sister died," Sally said.

"That doesn't mean -"

"It's *exactly* the same spot!" she said, looking up at him. "Are you seriously trying to tell me that's a coincidence?"

"I never said that, but -"

"It has to be linked to what happened tonight in the pub," she continued. "Whatever we unleashed, Matt, whatever we started... I don't think it's confined to the pub itself. I think it followed Jane and got her killed."

# CHAPTER TWENTY-ONE

"WE NEED TO FIGURE out what to do next," Matt said a short while later, as he led a shaken Sally into the pub and then turned to lock the door. "It'll be four in the morning soon. We can't let this go on all night."

He headed over to Sally and took her by the arm, trying to lead her to a seat, but after a moment she stopped and turned to look across the empty bar.

"Come on," Matt said, "we -"

"What do you want?" Sally screamed, pushing him away and stepping over to the middle of the room.

"Sally, I think -"

"Just tell us what you want!" she shouted at the top of her voice, turning and looking around for any sign of Mildred Weaver. "Jane's dead! Are you happy now? She's dead, just like you!" She looked the other way. "Is that what you want? Do you want revenge on anyone who's alive?"

She waited, but all she heard was silence.

"I don't think this is going to work," Matt suggested. "You can't just yell at a ghost and make it talk to you."

"Or is that just a side project?" she continued, thinking out loud now as she tried to understand what Mildred was after. "Why do you want Annie Ashton? You've both been dead for years. Why are you still chasing after her? What could be so important?"

Again, she waited, and then she stormed over to the hallway and looked up the stairs.

"Answer me, you bitch!" she shouted, before banging her fist against the wall in another desperate attempt to get Mildred to respond. "Don't you think you at least owe us an explanation? After all, it looks like we're the ones who woke you up and gave you another shot at this, so why don't you play nice and actually talk to us instead of trying to attack us all the time?"

She looked up toward the landing, but still she heard no response.

"Or are you just so pathetic," she continued, "that you can't even show your face?"

She waited, and now the silence of the house seemed somehow even louder, almost as if the silence itself was Mildred Weaver's final, infuriating response. Sally knew that the dead woman was lurking somewhere, that she was listening, and she realized after a moment that Mildred's strategy seemed to be simply to ignore everything and wait for Annie to show herself again.

"I think maybe," Matt said cautiously, "we should just get out of here."

Sally turned to him.

"I know that might be the coward's way out," he continued, "but this isn't our pub. You said it yourself, you don't even know why you're here anymore. Let's let Jerry figure it all out. Hell, the guy's barely even here, he might not even notice if there are some weird bumps and noises. And even if he does, it doesn't have to be our problem."

"We started this," Sally pointed out. "We have to finish it."

"Says who?"

"Me!" she snapped. "We can't just run away! Anyway, Jane ran, and look what happened to her!"

"She -"

"Don't tell me it wasn't connected!" she said angrily. "Don't even try, because we both know it's not true!" She paused, glaring at him, before letting out a heavy sigh. "Fine," she added, "if you want to go, then go. I'm not keeping you here, and you might even get a lucky break. After all, you don't have any dark secrets that might come back to haunt you, do you?"

"No, but..."

He thought for a moment about his mother's continued insistence that his father visited every night, and he realized that he could no longer be quite so certain that she was wrong.

"What do we do, then?" he asked. "I've got to tell you, I'm all out of ideas. Jane's dead, and I'm pretty sure I would be too if you hadn't interrupted Mildred while she was trying to strangle me in the cellar. It's obvious that she's dangerous and -"

Suddenly somebody knocked on the pub's front door. Sally and Matt both turned and looked back across the room, and then they turned to one another.

"Is that her?" Matt whispered.

"Knocking from outside?" Sally replied, also keeping her voice down. "That doesn't make much sense if -"

Before she could finish, the knocking returned, a little louder this time.

"It's probably the police," Matt pointed out. "I don't know about you, but I think maybe we should make sure there's no sign we've been having a lock-in first."

He stepped over to the table and grabbed the empty beer glasses, and then he carried them behind the bar and hid them out of sight.

"We can just say that we were woken by the sounds outside," he explained, clearly panicking a little, "and that we were about to go to bed. They might wonder why *I'm* here but, well, we can come up with some kind of story."

"I don't think the police would be going door-to-door just yet," Sally pointed out, as she stared at the door and tried to imagine who could possibly be out there. "What if it's..."

For a moment, she imagined Jane's mangled body, and she wondered whether somehow Jane might be trying to get back into the pub. If she opened the door, would she find her friend standing right outside? She figured that if ghosts were real, then it stood to reason that Jane might well be around somewhere, so she cautiously made her way to the window, telling herself that she had to be careful. After all, she blamed herself for allowing the spirit board into the pub in the first place.

Stopping for a moment, she carefully moved the blind aside and peered out. She could just about make out a dark figure on the step; she couldn't tell much about the person, but she was pretty sure that it wasn't Jane.

"Do you see anyone?" Matt asked.

"There's someone there and -"

The figure knocked again.

"And I'm pretty sure he's seen me," she

added, taking a step back. She turned to Matt, who was still behind the bar. "It's not a policeman, though. I'm pretty sure of that."

They stood in silence for a moment.

"Should we open it?" Matt asked.

"A third person might be useful," she pointed out. "We don't necessarily have to explain everything that's happened, but we can ask them if they'll join us using the spirit board. It could actually be a way out of this mess."

"Then I guess we should give it a try."

"On the other hand, we might be getting someone else unnecessarily involved. Is that fair?"

She hesitated, before stepping over to the door and pulling the bolt across. After taking a moment to pull herself together, she opened the door, only to find that there was nobody waiting outside.

She leaned out and looked both ways along the street, but there was still nobody.

"Did they leave?" Matt asked.

"I didn't hear footsteps," she replied, puzzled as she watched some nearby parked cars and waited in case somebody appeared. After a few seconds, figuring that perhaps some passing drunk had momentarily tried to get in, she turned to shut the door, only to see that a note had been left pinned to the wood.

Reaching up, she took hold of the note and

tore it away, before stepping back into the pub just as Matt came over.

"What have you got there?" he asked.

"Someone left this on the door," she told him, turning the note so that he could see it. "It's an address for a house on the other side of town. 119 Maddale Street. What do you think it means?"

Taking the note, Matt stared at it for a moment. Something about the note seemed vaguely familiar, although he couldn't quite put a finger on why he felt that way.

"I have no idea," he said finally, "but I don't think we can simply ignore it."

"That address is out past the old mill area," she pointed out. "It's in kind of a rough part of town. The few times I've been up there, I've been worried that someone might slash my tires at any moment. Why would someone want us to go out there? Anyway, it's the middle of the night, why would anyone be up at close to four in the morning?"

"I agree, it seems a little odd," he replied, still staring at the note and trying to figure out whether he'd really seen it somewhere before, "but to be honest, I'm all out of ideas. Let's face it, Sally, we're not exactly a promising pair of amateur ghost-hunters, and I really don't see us pulling something out of the bag at this late stage. And obviously *some* people are up, because someone put this on the door to begin with."

He turned to her.

"You've got a car, right?"

## CHAPTER TWENTY-TWO

"THERE'S A LIGHT ON," Sally pointed out as she switched the car's engine off and peered across the street. "That must be number 119, right?"

"I'm pretty sure it has to be," Matt replied, unfastening his seat-belt.

"I shouldn't even be driving," she said as she slipped out of the car, taking a step into a cold wind that was blowing in from the east. "Still, I feel sober as a rock right now." She looked over at Matt as he climbed out. "What do you think this is about?"

"Actually," he replied, "on the way over here, I had an idea. If I'm right, we might be about to meet someone who can tell us the truth about Mildred Weaver and *The Crowford Arms*."

\*\*\*

As Sally and Matt stood on the step, they listened to the sound of various locks and chains being turned and moved out of the way, before finally the door opened and they found themselves face-to-face with an elderly man.

"I've seen you before," Matt said immediately. "Out near the colliery yesterday morning."

"I'm really sorry to disturb you," Sally added, hoping to try a more conventional approach, "I hope we didn't wake you, but we saw that your light was on."

"I'm practically nocturnal these days," the man replied, adjusting his glasses as he peered at them both. He looked out toward the street, as if he was worried about someone else. "One can never be too careful, though. Not these days. This used to be such a nice area, but now there are all sorts of bad types roaming around, even at the dead of night." He turned to Sally again. "What did you say you were doing here?"

"I didn't," she said, before holding the note up. "Someone left this on the door of *The Crowford Arms* a little while ago."

"That's my address!"

"I know," she continued, "and to be honest, we wouldn't be out here so late if we weren't desperate."

"You're Ernest Dwyer, aren't you?" Matt said. "Someone was telling me about you today. You knew my father."

"I knew almost everyone's father at some point," Ernest replied. "I've lived in Crowford all my life. I don't remember meeting you at the colliery, but I do think that you look rather familiar." He adjusted his glasses again. "Fred. Fred Ford. Wait, Fred, is that you?"

"Fred Ford was my father," Matt told him. "He died nine years ago."

"I'm very sorry to hear that," Ernest said. "He was a good man. Well, probably. The problem with being my age is that it can be hard to remember the details."

"Do you know who Mildred Weaver is?" Sally asked.

"Mildred Weaver?" Ernest furrowed his brow. "Now, that's a name I haven't heard in a while. Of course I know who Mildred Weaver is, or who she *was*. Some facts I never forget, and Mildred Weaver died in 1947. That's thirty-seven years ago. I know that, because I happened to be at her funeral."

"We think..."

Sally hesitated, worried about how to explain without sounding like a complete maniac.

"This is pointless," she said finally, taking a step back. "I'm sorry we disturbed you, Mr. Dwyer, but -"

"We think we've disturbed Mildred Weaver's ghost," Matt said, interrupting her. "In the pub, I mean. We messed around with a homemade spirit board, for reasons I don't really want to go into right now, and it seems like we've woken her up or attracted her attention or something like that. And the thing is, she's apparently in a very bad mood and one person has already died tonight, and -"

He tilted his head to one side and tapped the sore patch on his neck.

"She also tried to kill me," he added. "She's looking for a little girl."

"Annie Ashton?"

"You know what we're talking about?" Sally asked.

"It's been a long time since I thought about that poor girl, but yes, I remember those days very well." He stepped aside. "You'd better come in. It's dangerous to be out too long in this part of town. You locked your car, didn't you?"

"I double-checked," Sally admitted as she entered the house and saw that there were books and papers piled on every surface.

"These were old miners' cottages," Ernest explained as he shut the door after Matt. "Not a lot of them are used for that purpose anymore, but they were originally built in the 1920's when the miners came flooding down to take up new jobs at the pit.

That's why you have these endless rows of red-bricked terraced houses, all built on the site of the old mill that shut down a few years before the pit opened. That's when Crowford really began to get bigger. Why, the town must have almost doubled in size in the years I've been alive." He began to shuffle slowly through to the kitchen. "Sorry, it takes me quite a while to get anywhere these days. Can I make anyone a cup of tea?"

"Thank you," Sally replied, "but we really don't have much time. We're trying to work out why Mildred Weaver's ghost is hunting Annie Ashton down, and whether there's anything we can do to stop her."

She paused for a moment.

"And believe me," she added, "I feel completely ridiculous saying those words out loud."

"It's been a long time since Annie Ashton went missing," Ernest replied.

"She went missing?" Matt said. "Like... disappeared completely?"

"I remember the scandal," Ernest said, as he stopped and leaned against the back of an armchair. "So many people were convinced that Mildred had killed the poor girl. Now, I was no particular fan of Mildred Weaver, I never even went into her pub very often, but I still thought that some of the things that were said about her were completely wrong. Now, when did Annie disappear? 1923, I believe.

Mildred was a widow by then, she and her husband Leonard had adopted the orphan girl but Leonard died soon after. Mildred was left running the pub by herself, and raising a little girl for whom she had no real affection."

"What happened to Annie?" Sally asked.

"She was only ten when she disappeared," Ernest continued. "I'm sure you can imagine the rumors that spread through this town like wildfire. Now, I love Crowford more than perhaps anyone alive, but even I have to admit that the people here can sometimes turn on someone in the ugliest manner imaginable. And they turned on Mildred, and many people refused to set foot in her pub again because they were convinced that she'd done something awful to the child. Mildred Weaver might have been a harsh woman, and she might have been cruel at times, but a murderer? No, I never believed that and I still don't today."

"Then where did Annie go?" Matt asked.

"That's the big question," Ernest said, nodding sadly.

"Mildred's still looking for her," Sally told him, "and Annie..."

She thought back to the message on the wall.

"And Annie's still hiding from her," she continued. "After all these years."

"I'm not surprised that Mildred wants to find

her," Ernest admitted. "To her dying day, she swore blind that she'd never hurt the girl, and that one day someone would come forward and reveal what had happened. She believed that Annie must have been abducted by someone and murdered. I've kept my ear to the ground, but I never heard of a young girl's bones being discovered anywhere, at least not a girl who could have been Annie. Mildred was still hated by many people when she died, still suspected of committing one of the most ghastly, unforgivable crimes imaginable. Killing a child."

Sally felt a shudder pass through her chest.

"We've woken her up," Matt said, "and we don't know what to do next. She killed our friend, and we're worried that she won't stop hurting people until she gets what she wants."

Ernest hesitated, before stepping around the armchair and taking a seat. He let out a pained groan as his aged knees creaked, and he took a moment to make himself comfortable.

"If you can help us in any way at all," Matt continued, "I'm begging you, we'll do anything. Someone obviously thought you might be able to tell us something, or they wouldn't have given us your address. We have to find a way to either silence Mildred Weaver's ghost, or get her to stop being so angry."

"It all started so very long ago," Ernest replied. "1923 was... what, sixty-one years ago? It's almost impossible to believe that so much time has passed. From what I understand, Mildred ran that pub with an iron fist, and she wasn't one to tolerate fools. By the time her husband had been dead a few years, she'd already come to despise the little orphan girl they'd adopted. Some say she even wanted her dead..."

# CHAPTER TWENTY-THREE

*1923...*

"GET OUT FROM UNDER my feet, girl!" Mildred Weaver roared, turning and grabbing Annie by the hair, then pushing her over to the other side of the bar area. "I won't tell you again!"

"I'm sorry," Annie said, struggling to hold back a giggle as she turned and looked over her shoulder. "I didn't mean to upset you."

"Go and fetch some empty glasses from the tables," Mildred said, pointing toward the far end of the pub. "Go, girl! Make yourself useful! Mind that you don't disturb people, though. And whatever you do, don't you dare touch those slops!"

As Annie hurried away, Mildred turned to the men who were sitting on their stools on the other side of the bar. Reaching down, she picked up a cigarette and took a long drag, and then she exhaled slowly. She glanced at the clock and saw that she still had several hours to go before she'd be able to throw everyone out.

"There's music at *The Red Cow* tonight," a man grumbled. "Ron Thurdle's playing his fiddle."

"Then go to *The Red Cow*!" Mildred barked angrily, before turning and seeing that Annie was talking to a man at a table. "Get working!" she roared, causing Annie to immediately hurry to another table. "Don't let me spot you slacking, girl!"

"You shouldn't be too hard on the little lass," Edward Osborne told her. "She's only young, and she needs to find an outlet for all that energy somewhere."

"She can get it out by working for me," Mildred muttered, as she tapped the head of the cigarette against an ashtray. "It was Len who was so keen on having a child in the house. He said that seeing as we didn't have any of our own, we should take in a stray. He promised he'd be the one to look after her, and that he'd be the one to discipline her, and all of that. And then what did he do?" She coughed for a moment, trying to clear her lungs as smoke swirled in the air all around the room. "He died, that's what," she continued, "and he left me with the pub and the child. I'm not sure which is worse."

"She seems bright," Edward observed.

"Too bright."

"And happy."

"Too happy."

"And she's still so young."

Mildred glared at him.

"I'm just saying that you should give her a chance," he added. "The poor thing's been though a lot over the past few years and she's still young enough to learn some good habits."

"She's been through nothing!" Mildred snapped. "She's just a child, she doesn't even have proper feelings! She's a naughty little girl who hasn't yet learned that the world is a wicked and cruel place! I'll tell you one thing, though, Edward Osborne... I swear on my husband's grave that I'll make sure she understands her place, and that she knows how lucky she is to have been allowed to live here. And if she refuses to learn those things, then I'll have no hesitation in slinging her back out onto the streets, where she can fend for herself."

"Come on, Mildred," Edward replied with a nervous smile, "you don't actually mean that, do you?"

"Every word," she sneered.

"I know you like to talk tough," he continued, "but I think I see a softer side to you. Don't laugh, it's true. I think that deep down, underneath it all, Mildred Weaver has a heart of gold. You just try to act tough so that people don't think you're a pushover."

"Rot!" she snapped.

"You could have turfed the girl out already," he replied. "You obviously try to look after her, and to educate her as well."

"The girl must eventually be good for something," she told him, unable to hide the sense of disapproval in her voice. "I'll whip her into shape, even if it's the last thing I ever accomplish in this life. Young people these days are little more than -"

Before she could finish, a loud crashing sound caused her to spin around, just as the last of the empty glasses slid off the tray Annie was carrying back through. The glass smashed against the floor, joining the others in a pile of broken shards.

"I'm sorry!" Annie gasped, clearly terrified that she was in yet more trouble. "I didn't mean -"

"You clumsy little oaf!" Mildred shrieked, rushing over to her and yanking the tray from her hands, before slapping her hard on the side of the face and then clipping her ear. "Don't you know how to do anything without causing trouble?"

"I'm sorry!" Annie sobbed. "I -"

"You're nothing but a pain!" Mildred sneered, before slapping her again. "Get out of my sight! When I come through to find you later, you'd best be prepared for a caning!"

Horrified, Annie turned and raced through to the hallway, leaving Mildred standing next to the pile of broken glass.

Turning, Mildred realized that everyone in the room had stopped to stare at her.

"Well?" she shouted. "What are you all gawping at me for? Don't you have drinks to be drinking? And if you don't, don't you have wives to be getting home to?"

\*\*\*

"Goodnight, Mildred," Edward muttered several hours later, as he put his hat on and stepped out onto the pavement. "Don't be too harsh on the young thing, will you? She's only a child, after all."

He turned to Mildred.

"We were all that age once," he added. "She was genuinely trying to help this evening. I think she just tried to carry too much at once, that's all."

"And by doing so," Mildred replied, "she made far more mess. I shall discipline the girl as I see fit, and I don't need any advice on that score. Thank you for your custom tonight, Edward. I hope to see you again soon".

"You know, if -"

"Goodnight, Edward," she said firmly. "Be told."

With that, she shut the door and slid the bolt across, and then she leaned back against the wall and put her head in her hands. For a moment, listening to the silence, she thought of all the work that she still had to get done, and of the fact that it would all start again the following day. And the day after that. And so on, forever. Sometimes she even though of selling up, but she knew she'd never make enough money to retire, even if she took the brewery's offer; she was chained to the pub, and she would remain chained to it until the day she inevitably keeled over from sheer exhaustion.

Lowering her hands, she took a moment to regather her composure, and then she marched across the room and stopped at the door to the hallway.

"Annie?" she called out, trying to take a little of the anger out of her voice. "Young lady, I want you to come down here this instant."

She waited, but she heard no reply.

"Annie, that's an order," she continued. "I won't tell you again. Come downstairs at once!"

Again, she heard no reply and no sign that the girl was moving.

"This is ridiculous," she muttered under her breath as she began to make her way upstairs. "The child can't even obey a simple instruction. If people knew what she was really like, they wouldn't admonish me for being so tough with her, they'd praise me for my patience."

She headed straight to the door to Annie's bedroom and pushed it open.

"Young lady -"

Stopping suddenly, she found that once again there was no sign of the girl. She checked under the bed, and now she was at a loss, for she felt certain that she'd have noticed if Annie had left the building. She had to be hiding somewhere, evidently playing yet another foolish game, one for which Mildred had no time whatsoever. After hesitating for a moment and listening for any sign of the girl's location, Mildred stepped back out onto the landing.

"Annie Ashton," she roared, "you will come here immediately. Do you hear me? I'm not going to come chasing after you, if that's what you think. You're ten years old and that's more than old enough for you to act like a mature young lady. Cease these childish games and come to get your punishment in a mature manner."

She listened again, and she could feel her blood boiling as she realized that the child was still hiding.

"Fine," she said, heading into her room and fetching the birch cane that she reserved for particularly serious infringements, "I have tried to be reasonable, but clearly you are in dire need of an urgent lesson. Annie, I'm warning you, if I have to come and root you out then your punishment will be worse by several orders of magnitude. This is your absolutely final chance to do the right thing."

Again she waited, filled with more rage than ever, but she was starting to realize that she'd have to drag the child kicking and screaming from whatever hiding place she'd chosen.

"Indeed," she purred finally, "you clearly have no shame whatsoever. I shall not enjoy the punishment that I must mete out, but I shall deliver it in the full knowledge that I have tried every alternative. My father caned me when I was a girl, and it did me no harm at all."

She made her way over to the spare room and pushed the door open, determined to find Annie as quickly as possible.

"I'm coming for you, girl," she announced firmly, "and when I find you, you're going to beg me for mercy as I lash you with this cane to within an inch of your miserable little life."

# CHAPTER TWENTY-FOUR

*1984...*

"FOR MORE THAN TWENTY years after that," Ernest continued, "Mildred Weaver searched for little Annie. Some say she became obsessed. Even as the rumors swirled, Mildred was determined to prove her innocence. But, of Annie Ashton, there was no sign."

"What if she ran away?" Matt asked. "Wouldn't that be the simplest explanation? Did anyone ever try to track her down?"

"Then her ghost wouldn't be in the pub," Sally pointed out.

"Exactly," Ernest said. "Mildred always suspected that Annie had never left the property, and now it sounds as if she was right. If the girl's ghost *is* there, then that makes it almost certain that she died either in the pub, or very close. The question, though, is where her body might rest now. Mildred searched high and low, it's hard to believe that the poor little corpse might have eluded her."

"So you don't have a problem believing in everything we've told you about what happened tonight?" Matt continued. "You believe that we've encountered these ghosts?"

"I've lived in Crowford for long enough to know that there are ghosts knocking about," Ernest said with a wry smile. "Of course, not everyone sees them. Actually *seeing* a ghost is something of an acquired ability. One might almost call it an art. Some people are born with a natural skill, some can't manage it no matter how hard they try. Most people, meanwhile, can learn to see ghosts, but they require some form of catalyst, some event that helps open their eyes."

"Like a session with a spirit board?" Matt asked.

"That might very well do the trick."

"Then we *are* to blame," Sally said, turning to Matt. "Those ghosts have been there all the time, but we just couldn't see them. No-one could. Until now."

"That doesn't necessarily mean that its our fault," he replied. "And what about Jane? You don't think that Mildred followed her and killed her, do you?"

"No, but the whole evening might have made Jane more able to see any other ghosts that were around her," she suggested. "What if her dead sister was haunting her all this time, and Jane wasn't able to see her until tonight?"

"And if you used a spirit board to contact the ghosts in that pub," Ernest continued, "then you opened a door that must be closed. This is a process that works in both directions. The ghosts don't tend to notice the living very much, not unless they're encouraged to do so. Once that has occurred, however, you must close the session properly."

"We tried, but she refused," Sally told him. "Could that be because there were three of us when we started, and only two at the end?"

"Indeed," Ernest said. "The two of you wouldn't be able to do it, especially if she's a strong ghost, and I imagine that Mildred Weaver would be stronger than most. You should be able to manage with a third person, though, but it's best to hurry." He began to get up. "I suppose there's really only one thing for it."

"You don't need to come!" Sally said, suddenly panicking.

"Do you have any other options?" Ernest asked.

Sally tried to think of an answer, before turning to Matt.

"Are you sure?" Matt asked, as he helped Ernest out of the chair. "It's so late, and -"

"And I'm a frail old man?" He chuckled. "I can't exactly argue with you, but I should point out that I can still get about. Besides, all we have to do is go in there and close the session, and that should be the end of the matter. We should hurry, though. The longer the session remains open, the more determined the spirit will be to remain. I'm sure I don't have to explain to either of you that it'd be best if Mrs. Weaver's ghost is discouraged from causing any further trouble."

Sally turned to Matt again, but he merely shrugged.

"Besides," Ernest added, "I don't get out of the house very much these days. I'd rather like to whizz into town and take a look around. Don't you think that sounds like fun?"

\*\*\*

"What color did you say it was again?" Matt asked as he leaned back into the car. "Brown?"

"Beige," Ernest told him with a knowing smile. "I'm sorry that I forgot it, but I'd really like to have that scarf with me, I try not to get too cold. I'd go myself but, well, you saw how long it took me to get from the house to the car. If you hurry, I'm sure you'll have no problem. You should find the scarf somewhere in the back room."

He reached out with a trembling hand and passed the key to Matt.

"Make sure you lock the door once you leave, though," he added. "There are people around here who wouldn't need a second invitation to break in. Two of my neighbors have been burgled in the past week alone. Honestly, sometimes I wonder what will become of this town. The decline in morality is shocking, and the poverty level seems to be rising all the time."

"I'll be back in a moment," Matt said, shutting the car door and then heading back over to the house.

"I do feel so very bad, asking him to go back in there," Ernest muttered, before turning to Sally. "And you, my dear, have an accent that suggests you're not born and bred in Crowford like the rest of us."

"I grew up in London," she told him.

"How lovely. My late wife and I used to take little trips up to see the galleries, and so that I could visit various national archives. Those days are long gone, of course, but I look back on them very fondly. London is such a fascinating and busy place, although I could never have lived there. It's far too hectic." He watched her for a moment. "What brought you to Crowford?"

"Oh..."

She paused as she tried to work out how much to tell him.

"My son and I moved here earlier this year," she admitted finally.

"And where is your son now?"

"He's..."

Again, she paused.

"He died," she said finally. "Not long after we arrived. He was eight."

"I'm very sorry to hear that," Ernest replied. "Children shouldn't die, it just seems so very wrong. I always wonder about the order of the universe when I hear of such things. But I don't think you mentioned *why* you and your son moved here. Do you have family in the area?"

"Nope," she replied, watching the house and hoping that Matt would emerge soon.

"So you came on a whim, did you?"

"Pretty much."

Still watching the house, she realized that Ernest was staring at her. In fact, she was starting to worry that somehow he was starting to guess that she'd had ulterior motives in moving to the town.

"I've never really been to this part of town before," she said, trying to change the subject. She was lying, but at least it was something to talk about. "It doesn't seem so bad."

"This was all once a big mill," he replied, "but that's been gone for some time now. So did you just stick a pin in a map and decide to move to wherever it landed?"

"More or less. I saw a fish and chip shop just around the corner. Is it any good?"

"It's fabulous. Crowford doesn't tend to receive much attention from the wider world. Is that what appealed to you? Were you looking for somewhere you could disappear?"

"It was a little more complicated than that."

"How so?"

She turned to him, and she realized in that moment that he definitely seemed unwilling to drop the subject. He either knew, or suspected, more than he was letting on.

"Please don't take this the wrong way," he continued, "but I sense great sadness in you. Not just because of your son's death, either. Something is eating away at your soul, and I fear that you're losing the battle with whatever it might be."

"I don't know what you're talking about," she replied, although she could hear that she sounded very unconvincing.

"You must find a way to deal with it," he said firmly, "because otherwise it will consume more and more of you until there's nothing left but emptiness and darkness and sorrow. I've seen that happen to people before, and it's always such a great tragedy. For you, however, I believe that there is still time. Not *much* time, but enough that you can still save yourself. I pray that you find your way."

She opened her mouth to reply, but for a few seconds she had no idea what to say. Then, spotting movement in the distance, she realized with relief that Matt was already on his way back from the house, and she spotted what appeared to be a scarf in his hands.

"Looks like we can get on our way," she told Ernest. "He's got your scarf."

"Scarf?" Ernest furrowed his brow, before looking out the window. "Ah, yes, of course. My scarf. I really wouldn't want to go anywhere without it."

## CHAPTER TWENTY-FIVE

"*THE CROWFORD HOY*," Ernest said, shortly before 5am, as he stepped through the door and looked around the empty bar area. "It has been a long time since I was last in here, but not much has changed. What's the new landlord's name?"

"Jerry," Sally told him. "Jerry Butler."

"He should make the place more his own," Ernest continued, as he shuffled over to the bar, leaning heavily on his cane. "A landlord should always try to do that, in my opinion. This room, for instance, doesn't appear to have changed one iota since I last visited." He paused, listening to the silence. "I might be imagining this," he added, "but I feel as if there is most certainly a presence here. I can well believe that the ghost of Mildred Weaver is somewhere close."

"The spirit board was damaged earlier," Matt said, shutting the door and then hurrying over to the table. "I taped it back together, though. Will that be okay?"

"I imagine so."

"It's also a rather unconventional design. It's homemade. Would that be a problem?"

"I don't see why," Ernest replied. "Would you mind popping another log onto the fire?"

Sally headed over and added two more logs. She took a moment to warm her hands, and then she turned to see that Ernest was looking up toward the ceiling.

"She's waiting," he said after a moment. "For little Annie, I mean. The sense of expectation is palpable, she wants to prove – if nothing else – that she didn't murder the girl. I imagine poor Mildred has been driven quite insane over the years. You told me that you'd seen Annie, did you not?"

"She wrote a message on the wall upstairs. I can show you, if you want."

"That's not necessary. Clearly she's still hiding after all these years, and I can't say that I entirely blame her. Mildred could be a most formidable woman for anyone to deal with, especially a little girl."

"If we close the session with the spirit board," Sally replied, "what happens to Annie?"

Ernest turned to her.

"She's already dead," he pointed out. "What more *can* happen to her?"

"Will she just be trapped here forever, always trying to hide from Mildred? Are we actually going to help her, or are we just trying to make it so that we don't see the problem?"

"I'm not entirely sure that we can help the child," Ernest told her. "If we knew where to find her body, we might be able to do something, but it's hard to believe that we'd have much luck. After all, Mildred searched high and low and found nothing. That's what makes this all so difficult to understand. If the girl died on the property, then what happened to her body?"

"We can't just consign Annie to eternity being pursued by that woman," Sally told him. "It's wrong."

"Perhaps, but I'll say this again, I don't know how to help her. We can't win every battle, my dear." He took a deep breath. "But we *can* undo what you've done tonight, and we can at least make sure that the living are protected from Mildred's anger."

"We can't save the world," Matt said. "Sally,

let's just get this done."

She opened her mouth to argue with him, but at the last moment she realized that he was right. Looking around, she knew that they couldn't rip the pub apart in search of the dead girl's body, and she also knew that Annie had shown no sign that she wanted to reveal the location of her final resting place. Even though she hated the idea of leaving the girl at the mercy of Mildred Weaver, Sally finally turned to Ernest as she accepted that they'd hit a dead end.

"Let's set the spirit board up," Ernest said as he shuffled to the table and took a seat. "Just the way you did it before will be fine, there's no need for anything fancy."

Still looking around in case she spotted any sign of Annie, Sally headed over to join him.

"I should have asked her when I had the chance," she said, unable to hide the sense of sadness in her voice. "I should have realized."

"Sit down, my dear," Ernest said, patting the seat of the next chair along. "Please."

As she and Matt took their positions, Sally looked at the spirit board and thought about how eager she'd been all those hours earlier; she'd never seriously considered the possibility that the board might be dangerous, and now her friend was dead and she'd seen final, incontrovertible proof that ghosts were real. In just a matter of hours, her entire world had been turned upside down, and she'd failed to get the one thing she'd been after in the first place. She hadn't made contact with Tommy.

"Everybody touch the marker," Ernest said calmly.

"Have you done this before?" Matt asked.

"Maybe once or twice," he replied with a faint smile. "Usually with more conventional boards than this one. Come on, let's get started."

They each placed a fingertip on the marker, and then Sally and Matt waited for Ernest to take the lead.

"I can't believe we're doing this," Matt muttered. "This has been the craziest night."

"Spirits," Ernest said, watching the board keenly, "I'm afraid we must take our leave of you. Whatever has transpired tonight, I hope you will understand that nobody acted with malice. Nobody sought to harm anyone. Two worlds mixed tonight, worlds that should stay separate, and -"

Before he could finish, they all heard a faint bumping sound from the far side of the room.

"Stay focused," Ernest told Sally and Matt. "This won't work as well if you're distracted."

"I'm focused," Matt replied. "Believe me,

I've never been more focused on anything in my entire life."

"Spirits, we bid you farewell," Ernest continued. "We are not -"

Suddenly a brief cry rang out from somewhere upstairs.

"That's her!" Sally gasped, getting to her feet.

"Put your finger back on the marker," Ernest said firmly. "We're so close now."

Hearing the sound of footsteps, Sally tried to follow them as they hurried across the floor of the room directly above.

"It's Annie," she said cautiously. "Mildred must be close to catching her again."

"Please," Ernest said, "you must -"

Another bump broke the silence, and this time Sally looked over at the door to the cellar.

"I don't get it," she said after a few seconds. "You guys are hearing this as well, aren't you?"

"I'm telling you," Ernest said, "you must sit down immediately. Every second that passes is another second that the task becomes harder. You can't do anything to help Annie or Mildred. All you can do is close the session so that the world of the living is no long affected by these ghosts."

"She must be terrified," Sally said, before

hearing another thud from the cellar door. She looked over, and this time she saw that a piece of wood had appeared on the floor. "What the hell *is* that?" she asked as she hurried over.

"Sally, get back here!" Matt called out.

Reaching down, Sally picked up the chunk of wood, which turned out to be nothing more than a rotten little lump. She reached through and switched the light on, and then she looked down the steps just in time to see another piece of wood slide into view.

"Hurry!" Ernest shouted.

"Something's happening," she replied. "It's like -"

Before she could say another word, the piece of wood at the bottom of the stairs began to turn, until its jagged edge was pointing into the cellar itself.

"It's like a message," she continued, as she began to realize what was happening. "I think someone's trying to tell us something about the cellar!"

"I've been down there," Matt reminded her, as they all heard more footsteps coming from somewhere upstairs. "Sally, this isn't the time to start exploring. We need to help Ernest shut this whole thing off right now!"

"I'm going to take another look," she replied, as she began to make her way down the stairs. "I'll only be a couple of minutes, but I have to give Annie one last chance. I think she might be trying to tell us something!"

"Sally, no!" Matt shouted, and then he sighed as he turned back to Ernest. "Sorry, I guess she's pretty stubborn. She still thinks she can help Annie before we end this madness."

"I can feel Mildred's presence," Ernest replied, looking around the room for a moment before glancing up at the ceiling. "She's close, and she knows that we're here. Most likely, she also knows exactly what we're trying to do. If she thinks that we're threatening her in any way, she'll try to stop us, so it would be wise to proceed with haste."

"Exactly how many times have you done this, again?" Matt asked.

Ernest turned to him.

"Too many times," he said firmly. "That doesn't matter now. What matters is that we end this session with the spirit board before anyone else gets hurt."

# CHAPTER TWENTY-SIX

"COME ON, ANNIE," Sally whispered, standing in the cellar and looking around, waiting for another sign, "you wanted me to come down here. Why?"

Hearing a bumping sound, she turned to her left. Several kegs were piled up in the corner, and for a moment Sally felt as if – out of the corner of her eye – she'd spotted a hint of movement.

Cautiously, she made her way across the cellar, approaching the kegs and keeping an eye out for the ghostly little girl.

"It's okay," she continued. "You met me before. You remember that, don't you? We were upstairs, and you gave me a message. I didn't understand it at the time, but I think I do now. Annie, are you trying to show me where your body's hidden? Is that what you want? Do you want it to be found after all these years?"

Reaching the corner, she looked behind the kegs, but all she saw was an empty space. A moment later, however, a spade fell down against the floor. Startled, Sally turned, just in time to see the spade spin around until it was pointing toward the opposite corner.

"Over there?" she said out loud, still hoping to get Annie to actually speak. "Is that where you want me to look?"

She waited for a moment, in case she heard an answer, and then she walked over to the other corner. All she saw was a bare wall, with a few bricks missing near the top. She looked down at the floor and saw a large crack, but there was nowhere for anybody to hide. Frustrated, she realized that the little girl was probably still terrified of attracting Mildred's attention.

"You know," she continued, "if you want me to do something, you could just say it, instead of offering me all these vague clues."

Suddenly something bumped against her from behind, pushing her into the corner. She immediately turned to look, and for a fraction of a second she thought she could hear footsteps, but silence quickly fell again.

"Annie, is this where I'm supposed to look? I don't see anything, but is this where your body's hidden?"

Realizing that she wasn't going to get a proper reply, she turned to look at the corner again. There was really nowhere to search, although after a few seconds she looked up at the missing bricks and tried to figure out whether a child could ever have fitted through that space. The idea seemed improbable, but after a moment she realized that there might just be a chance. She looked around and spotted a chair over by some of the kegs; after pulling the chair closer, she climbed up and began to examine the gap in the wall. Cobwebs covered the empty space, but after moving those aside she peered a little closer.

All she saw, however, was darkness.

Remembering the flashlight at the top of the steps, she climbed off the chair and hurried back across the room.

\*\*\*

"What's taking her so long?" Matt muttered, looking toward the cellar door again but quickly realizing that there was no point calling out to Sally. "She's never going to find anything."

He turned to Ernest.

"It's getting really late now," he pointed out. "Do we need to get this done by the time the sun comes up, or something like that?"

"Ideally, yes," Ernest replied, staring at him

with a curiously calm expression.

"That still gives us about an hour," Matt said, although he couldn't help looking over his shoulder again, still waiting for Sally to return. "She's wasting time down there. Do you think I should go and make her come back up?"

"You certainly could."

Matt looked back over at him. He opened his mouth to ask another question, but at that moment he realized that Ernest suddenly seemed different somehow, a little stilted, as if he'd become more troubled than before.

"Are you okay?" Matt asked.

"Me?" Ernest hesitated. "I'm fine, although I must confess that I'm a little startled by the sight of Annie Ashton."

"By the..."

Matt's voice trailed off for a moment.

"Where?" he asked.

"Right next to you."

Matt opened his mouth to ask again what he meant, but then – turning to his left – he realized that someone was indeed standing just beyond his shoulder. He turned all the way, and then he let out a shocked gasp as he found himself face-to-face with the dead little girl.

Suddenly a thud hit the floor of the room above, causing Annie to turn and run. Matt watched as she raced around the fireplace and dropped down to hide behind the brick edge, and then he looked back over at Ernest.

"She's truly remarkable," Ernest said, his voice filled with wonder. "I've seen ghosts before, but never one that's quite as clear and vivid as this one. There's so much I want to ask her, although I know that this isn't exactly the right moment. She's astonishing, though. She's so... present."

Another thud hit the floor above.

"She's not the only one," Matt pointed out as he looked up toward the ceiling, and a moment later he heard the unmistakable sound of somebody stepping out onto the landing. "I think Mildred knows that something's up."

As those words left his lips, he heard a series of creaks coming from the hallway, and he realized that Mildred was slowly making her way down the stairs.

"Sally?" he called out, looking over toward the cellar door again. "I don't mean to rush you, but now would be a really good time to think about coming back up!"

He turned to Ernest again.

"I don't even know if she can hear me down there."

"Be a good sport," Ernest replied, "and go and fetch her, will you?" The footsteps were still moving down the stairs, getting closer. "I've never been much of a one for panicking, but I must admit that this is cutting things rather fine."

Matt turned and looked at Annie for a moment, watching as she tried to squeeze herself further out of sight. Then, realizing that the footsteps had reached the hallway, he got to his feet and turned to go over to the cellar door. Before he managed to get any further, however, he saw Mildred Weaver's ghostly figure step into view over by the far end of the bar.

In an instant, he remembered the sensation of her cold, dead hands wrapped around his throat. Pulling back against the wall, he felt the fear starting to tighten in his chest.

"There she is," Ernest said, before swallowing hard. "I have to say, she really hasn't changed much." He turned to Matt. "Would you mind hurrying up, young man?"

For a few seconds, Matt was frozen in place by the sight of Mildred's ghost. Finally, however, he began to edge toward the cellar door, just as Mildred took another step forward. The air all around her became noticeably colder.

Suddenly Annie raced out from behind the bricks and ducked down behind one of the tables in the far corner of the room, desperately trying to stay out of sight.

"Sally!" Matt yelled. "Hurry!"

"There's no time," Ernest said, as he re-positioned the board. "Get back here, I have another idea!"

Matt hesitated, before making his way over to the table, where Ernest had already placed a fingertip on the marker.

"You said two people wouldn't be enough," Matt reminded him.

"Desperate times call for desperate measures," Ernest pointed out. "It might work. Or it might at least slow her down."

Matt reached out and touched the marker.

"Spirit, it's time to say goodbye," Ernest said firmly as Mildred made her way closer. "Let's get this over with."

He and Matt moved the marker over to the word Farewell and waited. Mildred walked calmly to the board and looked down, her expression filled with the most pitiful degree of contempt. For a moment the only sound in the room came from logs crackling in the fireplace.

"Is... is it working?" Matt asked, staring at the marker, too terrified to look up at Mildred's face. "Why isn't anything happening?"

He glanced at Ernest, hoping that the old man knew what he was doing.

"Spirit," Ernest said again. "Goodbye."

"At least it's not a definite no this time," Matt pointed out, allowing himself a glimmer of hope. "Not yet, anyway."

"Goodbye," Ernest continued. "Spirit, this

can go on no longer. We're leaving now. Goodbye."

Again, they waited. The air all around the table was so cold now, and Matt couldn't help looking over at the far corner and watching as Annie Ashton's ghost tried to hide behind some of the chairs. He wanted to help her, but he knew that their only hope was to use the spirit board and end the session forever.

"Okay," Matt said, "maybe -"

Suddenly the entire board flew off the table, breaking free and crashing into the fireplace, where it landed in the flames.

"Is that bad?" Matt asked, waiting for Ernest to say something, before finally looking up at Mildred Weaver's ghost, just as she looked toward the cellar door and then faded from sight. "What are we supposed to do now?"

## CHAPTER TWENTY-SEVEN

"HOW COULD YOU EVER fit through here?" Sally muttered, standing on the chair and aiming the flashlight through the hole at the top of the wall. "How could you even climb up?"

As she reached her right arm further through the gap and tilted the flashlight, she began to realize that while it seemed improbable that Annie might have squeezed her way into the space behind the wall, she might actually have been able to manage. The space would have been a good hiding place, and it wasn't beyond the realm of possibility that Mildred would never have thought to look in such an unlikely spot.

Standing on tiptoes, Sally craned her neck to get a better view. Finally, just as she was about to give up, she realized she could just about see something white down in the gap.

"Is that you?" she whispered, adjusting the flashlight again. "Annie, is -"

Suddenly she let out a gasp as she realized that she could see one side of a skull, with wisps of pale hair still clinging to some patches on the top. Shocked, she almost stepped straight back off the chair, but she forced herself to keep looking as she tilted the flashlight again and saw that the bottom of the skull seemed to be caught on something.

Hearing a shuffling sound, she looked over her shoulder.

"I think I found you," she said, even though she couldn't see Annie anywhere. "I'm not going to leave you trapped here forever with that woman, I just..."

Looking over at the far end of the cellar, she spotted various tools.

"I'm going to get you out of here," she continued, before climbing down from the chair and hurrying over to take a look. "I just need to figure out how."

Pulling various spades and trowels aside, she finally found a sledgehammer. She hauled it onto her shoulder and rushed back to the corner, and then she stared at the wall for a moment as she tried to figure out how she was going to break through. She knew that even if she succeeded, she'd still have to get the girl's body out, but she told herself that there'd be time to come up with the next part of the plan later. She briefly considered calling for Matt's help, although as she looked at the wall she realized that it seemed to be crumbling in places, which gave her hope.

"Here goes nothing."

After raising the sledgehammer, she swung it with all her strength, sending the head crashing against the wall.

Immediately, several bricks cracked and some small chunks crumbled and fell to the floor. Realizing that she actually had a chance, Sally swung again, and this time she was able to dislodge an even larger section of the wall. She swung the sledgehammer several more times, until finally she was able to see a section of the skeleton, at which point – worried that she might smash the girl's body – she leaned the sledgehammer against the wall and used her bare hands to start pulling some more of the loose bricks aside.

"I see you," she said as she managed to spot the girl's skull, which was partly impaled on a metal hook that ran up through the underside of the jaw. "What happened to you?" she continued. "Did you climb down there to hide, but you slipped and..."

For a moment, she imagined the poor girl falling in the tight, confined space. If the hook had pierced the underside of her jaw and broken through into her mouth, she would have been trapped; if she'd been knocked out, she could have simply bled to death. Either that, or she'd never have been able to call for help in time. Sure enough, some of the brickwork behind the skull seemed to be stained with something dark.

"Annie," she whispered, as she began to reach through to pull the skull clear. "You poor -"

Suddenly she heard another rustling sound over her shoulder. She turned, half expecting to see Annie's ghost, but instead she was horrified by the sight of Mildred Weaver.

\*\*\*

"Where did she go?" Matt asked, getting to his feet and looking all around. "Did it work? Did we make her leave?"

"I fear not," Ernest replied, "but I don't know why she would have -"

Before he could finish, Sally screamed in the cellar.

"I'm coming!" Matt shouted, rushing to the door, only for it to slam shut before he could get through. He immediately grabbed the handle and tried to pull it open again, but this time he found that some invisible force was keeping it firmly in place.

Sally's cries began to fade, and Matt couldn't help thinking back to the moment when Mildred had almost choked him to death.

"Sally!" he shouted, as he slammed his fists against the door. "Hold tight, I'm going to get you out of there!"

He looked around for something he could use to break the door down. Spotting nothing, he took a few steps back and then threw himself against the door, trying to smash his way through using his shoulder. To his surprise, however, the door was surprisingly sturdy, and he let out a grunt of pain as he fell back and hit the bar.

"What the hell is that thing made of?" he muttered, before launching himself at the door again, only to find that it once more failed to yield.

"There has to be another way to end this," Ernest said, as he shuffled over to the fireplace and used his cane to try to pull the spirit board clear of the flames. Already, the board's edges were starting to blacken and curl.

"She's going to kill Sally!" Matt shouted, trying the handle again, still finding that the door was fixed firmly in place.

"We need three people," Ernest continued, finally managing to get the board to the edge of the fire. Although the board was badly burned around the edges, the central section was still just about intact. "We need..."

His voice trailed off for a moment as he began to come up with the first vestiges of a new plan.

"Matthew!" he called out finally, turning and looking back across the room. "Get here now! I know what to do!"

"I have to get Sally out of the cellar!" Matt replied.

"There's only one way to stop Mildred Weaver," Ernest said firmly, "and that means using this thing."

"You said it yourself, we need three people!"

Setting the board on the floor, Ernest winced as he slowly began to kneel. Leaning heavily on his cane, he let out a gasp of pain.

"We *have* three people," he muttered, before looking over at Annie's ghost as she continued to hide behind the table and chairs in the far corner. "Sort of. Annie, I know you can hear me, and I know you're scared, but there's a way to end all of this and keep you safe at the same time. If you say goodbye to Mildred with us, there's a chance that you'll be severing any connection you might have with her. I can't guarantee that it'll work, but it's the only option right now."

He held a hand out toward her.

"Annie, please."

Still hiding, Annie turned and looked at him, her terrified face just about visible from behind the chairs.

"Annie," he said again, as Matt hurried back over to the board. "I'm begging you."

Annie stared at him for a moment longer, before finally turning and starting to crawl out. She got to her feet, but then she hesitated again as she looked around for any sign of Mildred's return.

"We have to hurry!" Ernest told her. "While she's distracted! Please, look past your fear and help us!"

"She's killing Sally!" Matt shouted at the girl. "Even if you won't do this for us, can't you do it for her?"

Annie stared at the board for a moment longer, before taking a step forward.

Suddenly Mildred Weaver's ghost reappeared right in front of the terrified girl, causing her to immediately turn and run. Mildred rushed after her, but Annie clambered back behind the table and then faded from view. As Mildred screamed and pulled the chairs aside, Matt turned and looked around the room.

"We have to find her!" he stammered. "Where did she go?"

"She's right here," Ernest said.

Turning, Matt saw that Annie was now kneeling in front of the board, and he watched as she reached out and touched the marker with a finger. Ernest immediately did the same, and then Matt dropped to his knees and added his finger too, just as Mildred's ghost rushed at the three of them.

"Spirit!" Ernest shouted. "It's time to go! Goodbye!"

With that, they moved the marker together to the word Farewell, and then they all turned and looked just as Mildred snarled and lunged at Annie. Just as her hand was about to reach the girl's throat, however, Mildred's ghost vanished from sight and her angry cry faded into the cold air. Annie flinched and began to pull away, before realizing that the woman was gone.

A fraction of a second later, the cellar door finally creaked open.

# CHAPTER TWENTY-EIGHT

"SALLY!" MATT SHOUTED AS he rushed down the stairs. "Sally, can you hear me?"

As soon as he reached the bottom, he saw that Sally was slowly getting to her feet on the far side of the cellar. He raced over to help her, and then – as he made sure she was steady – he looked at the nearby wall and saw that it had been smashed open to reveal parts of a little skeleton.

"What the..."

"It's her," Sally gasped, reaching up and touching her neck, which bore sore patches that had been caused by Mildred's icy grip. "It's Annie."

"Are you sure?" he asked, although he immediately realized that the question was somewhat foolish. "I guess... Who else could it be, right?"

"I think she climbed in there to hide from Mildred all those years ago," Sally explained, "but she must have fallen in the dark. There was some kind of hook poking out and it caught her jaw. She must have been knocked out, or maybe the hook meant she couldn't call for help. And then she bled to death." She turned to Matt. "We have to get the bones out of here. Mildred might come back at any moment."

"Mildred's gone."

"Are you sure?"

"We took care of it. We closed the session, with a little help from Annie herself."

"That explains why Mildred suddenly left me alone. She must have sensed what you were doing up there."

"So Annie's body has been down here all this time, huh?" Matt said, unable to stop looking at the bones. After a moment, he spotted the skull and saw that the jaw was still hooked on the piece of metal that jutted out from the wall. "I'm not about to try to rehabilitate Mildred or anything like that, but I guess she was right about one thing. She didn't murder the kid."

"Most people thought she did, though," Sally pointed out. "I kind of understand how that must have driven her out of her mind."

\*\*\*

"Something seems different, don't you think?" Ernest said as he picked up the damaged spirit board and dusted away a few flakes of ash. "The atmosphere here feels... more free, somehow."

"So Annie was able to take part in the session?" Sally asked as Matt helped her over to the table. "Even though she was dead?"

"The remains in the cellar will have to be taken away and examined," Ernest continued, "but it's hard to believe that they don't belong to the little girl. Once they're out of the pub, it's possible that her ghost will leave too, although I have a hunch that she might stick around. Now that she's said goodbye to Mildred, any connection between them has been severed and she should be left alone. Besides, Mildred will hopefully rest in peace now that her innocence has been demonstrated."

"I actually feel sorry for her," Matt admitted. "In a way. I mean, people really thought that she'd killed Annie. She was accused of doing one of the worst things imaginable."

Sally looked at him, and then she turned away.

"This should not be left out in the open," Ernest muttered, shuffling over to the fireplace and tossing the board into the flames, then watching as it burned away. "It might look like a toy, but it's not. I hope we've all learned tonight that communicating with the dead is seldom a good idea. And now, if you don't mind, it's getting very late and the sun will be coming up soon. Would someone mind giving me a lift home?"

"Would you mind taking him?" Sally asked, fishing the car keys from her pocket and handing them to Matt. "I just need to sit down for a few minutes. After all, Mildred Weaver almost strangled me."

"Are you sure you don't want to go to the hospital?" Matt asked.

"No, I'll be fine, but I don't think I'm quite up to driving. And I'll be okay alone here now. I could do with some time to figure things out."

"I'll be quick," he told her. He wanted to say more, but he figured that he could save that for later. "When I get back," he added, "we'll call the cops and tell them everything. After more than half a century, the mystery of little Annie Ashton's disappearance has finally been solved."

"Yeah," she said, with a hint of sadness in her voice. "We did it."

***

"Do you know something?" Ernest said half an hour later, as Matt helped him into the armchair at his house on Maddale Street. "I might actually be a little tired. I think I might take a little nap in a minute."

"Is there anything I can do for you before I go?" Matt asked.

"No, you've done enough already, dragging me out on this grand adventure." He reached out and patted the side of Matt's arm. "Thank you for that. Sincerely. I don't venture out much these days, but it was good to get the blood pumping again. You should probably warn the landlord, however, that he might notice a few extra unusual moments for a while. Even though we dealt with Mrs. Weaver's ghost, any other spirits in the building might be a little easier to spot for a few years. I wouldn't mind betting that *The Crowford Hoy* becomes something of a hub for supernatural activity in the town."

"I don't know what we'd have done without you," Matt replied, before taking the note from his pocket and looking once again at the strangely familiar handwriting. "Do you have any idea who might have left this for us? Whoever they were, they seemed to know that we needed help."

"Let me take a look," Ernest muttered, peering more closely at the note. "Do you see the curve on the letter M there? It's not definitive, of course, but I recall seeing that several times before. It was a curious habit of men from the colliery to write like that. At least, the first few generations who'd come down from the north."

"Men from the colliery?" Matt paused.

"Then what -"

Before he could finish, he realized exactly where he'd seen the handwriting before. He stared down at the note in astonishment, telling himself that he had to be wrong, but with each passing second he felt more and more certain that he was right.

"Do you recognize it now?" Ernest asked.

"It looks like my father's writing," he said cautiously, "but it can't be. I mean, he's been dead for years."

"I would have thought that if tonight has taught you anything," Ernest replied, "it's that the dead are still sometimes able to interfere in the affairs of the living. Sometimes helping out, sometimes causing trouble, even if we don't necessarily know that they're there."

"But..."

Matt stared at the note for a moment longer, before turning to Ernest again.

"I saw men at the pit," he said after a few seconds. "Yesterday morning. You were there too, and I saw men down there at the pit even though I know the place is empty during the strike."

"I have no doubt that all of those things happened exactly as you described them," Ernest replied.

"But... how?" Matt asked.

"Not all ghosts are there to be seen, or to

take revenge," Ernest explained. "I don't remember encountering you out there, but that doesn't mean that we didn't meet. It simply means that time can shift a little. I can't claim to entirely understand how that happens, but the important thing is to be open to the possibilities." He looked at the note again. "I remember meeting your father out there once, and you *do* look a lot like him. I suppose it's possible that a little confusion seeped in. These things can happen, especially close to the end of a life. And I must accept that my time will soon draw to a close."

"Did my father really leave this tonight?" Matt asked. "To help us?"

"That's certainly possible. All that really matters now is that the session with the spirit board is closed, and that the people who opened that session were able to say goodbye properly. Now, you can tell me to mind my own business if you like, but don't you have a rather lovely young lady to get back to?"

"I do," Matt replied. He still had so many questions, but he was starting to realize that he might not get many answers from the old man. "You're right, I should go and make sure that she's okay."

He headed to the door, but then he hesitated as he thought back to something Ernest had said. At first he didn't want to bring the matter up, but a niggling sense of fear was starting to rise through his chest.

"You said that the people who opened the session were able to say goodbye to Mildred Weaver properly," he said, turning to Ernest again, "but... technically, I'm the only one who was present both times. Jane's dead and Sally was down in the cellar. Does it matter that Sally didn't say goodbye to Mildred's ghost?"

Ernest stared at him for a moment, and slowly a sense of dread began to cross his features.

"Go back there immediately!" he barked. "Don't wait for me! Go back to the pub and get her out before it's too late!"

# CHAPTER TWENTY-NINE

STEPPING INTO HER ROOM at *The Crowford Hoy*, Sally stopped for a moment as she realized that she wasn't alone. She listened, trying to work out what had alerted her to a presence nearby, but all she heard was silence.

"Hello?" she said cautiously.

She looked around, but there was still no sign of anyone else in the room.

"You don't have to be scared anymore," she added. "I promise I won't hurt you."

Ever since Matt had left with Ernest Dwyer, Sally had been tidying the pub, hoping to make sure that Jerry would notice nothing amiss whenever he eventually returned. She'd more or less succeeded, although a few matters – such as the scratched message on the wall, and the damage in the cellar –

would have to be explained. She'd begun to feel strangely calm, as if getting on with actual work had helped mark an end to the night's strange activities. Now, however, she felt that flickering hint of doubt in her mind as she wondered whether a ghostly little presence might yet remain.

"Annie?" she whispered. "If you're here, it's okay to let me know."

She hesitated, and then – feeling as if she was being watched – she slowly turned and saw the ghostly figure of Annie Ashton standing in the doorway that led to one of the other rooms.

"Hey," Sally said softly.

Annie stared at her and, after a moment, furrowed her brow.

"You were very brave tonight," Sally continued. "You must have been scared."

"Is she gone?" Annie asked cautiously.

"I think she might still be around," Sally explained, "but she won't be able to hurt you. I don't think she'll be able to hurt anyone, she'll just sort of drift through the rooms, separated from the living and the dead. That's how I understand it, at least. The important thing is that you said goodbye to her, and Mr. Dwyer says that means she can't hurt you anymore."

She paused for a moment, worried about scaring the girl away, and then she took a step forward. Although Annie flinched, she didn't run away, so Sally edged a little closer before crouching down in front of her. For a few seconds, she could only stare into the eyes of the dead girl and marvel at what she was seeing; she knew that Annie had been dead for something like sixty years, and she also knew that seeing her at all was some kind of miracle. She wanted to reach out and touch her, but she managed to restrain herself.

"I want you to know," she continued, "that we're going to get some people to come and take your bones out of the wall. They'll be very careful and very respectful, but they'll probably want to run some tests on them."

"What kind of tests?" she asked.

"I don't exactly know, but they'll want to make sure that it's really you."

"It's really me," she replied. "I remember what happened."

"Was it quick?" Sally asked. "Was it painless?"

"No," Annie said. "It hurt a lot. I couldn't call for help. I couldn't climb out. I couldn't do anything. All I could do was hang there in the dark and hope that someone found me. I heard Mildred shouting my name for days, and slowly I started to get weaker. She was trying really hard to find me, and sometimes she was right on the other side of the wall. I even heard her taking a look at the gap, but I think she didn't really believe that I could have fitted through. I was so hungry and cold and scared but... that's okay. It was a long time ago now."

"After the tests are over," Sally continued, "we'll make sure that your bones are properly buried. Would you like that?"

Annie thought for a moment, before nodding.

"And where would you like to be buried?"

"Somewhere pretty," Annie told her. "I don't know anything about my parents, I don't remember them, so... Can I be buried in a big field, where there are lots of flowers? And butterflies! I love butterflies so much!"

"I'll make sure that happens," Sally replied. "I promise. There'll be a little stone with your name on it, so that people remember you. To be honest, I think the story of what happened to you is going to be pretty big news in Crowford for a while. People always love a mystery, and your story is pretty crazy. It's all over now, though. Aren't you happy that you were found eventually?"

Annie considered the question, before smiling as she nodded again.

"Thank you for trusting me," she continued. "When I realized that you were trying to show me where to find your body, I had to try to find you. The original plan was to just end the session, but that might have meant that everything would have just gone back to how it was before. I hated the idea of leaving you trapped here with Mildred Weaver again."

"That's okay," Annie replied, "but..."

She paused.

"It wasn't me who showed you," she added finally.

"It wasn't?" Sally replied. "Then who was it?"

"It was Tommy."

Sally felt an immediate punch of anticipation in her chest.

"What do you mean?" she asked. "Have you *seen* Tommy?"

"He's my new friend," Annie explained. "I know he's your son. He's been my friend since he died, we played a lot whenever Mildred wasn't around. Sometimes he's near you, but you never seem to notice him."

"Where is he now?" Sally stammered, getting to her feet and looking around. "Tommy, are you here?"

"He's not here right now," Annie told her. "I don't know where he is. He might have been scared off by Mrs. Weaver. I know he didn't like her much, even though she never tried to hurt him. I'm sure he'll be back soon, when he realizes that she's gone."

"Tommy!" Sally shouted, filled with panic as she realized that her son's ghost might be nearby.

"Tommy, it's me! Tommy, you have to talk to me!"

A moment later, she heard a creaking sound coming from one of the other rooms.

\*\*\*

As soon as he'd switched off the car's engine, Matt scrambled out and hurried along the pavement, heading toward the pub. Reaching the front door, he pushed it open and raced inside, and then he began to look around for Sally. His heart was pounding, and he knew that he had to find some way to get her to safety.

"Sally!" he shouted. "Where are you?"

"Up here!" she called back to him from one of the upstairs rooms. "I'm looking for Tommy! I think he might actually be here!"

"You have to get out of the pub," he replied, hurrying through to the hallway and looking up the stairs. "Sally, I'll explain later, but for now I have to get you away from this place while we figure out what to do next!"

Stepping into view at the top of the stairs, Sally looked down at him and smiled.

"What are you on about?" she asked. "Everything's fine, but Annie told me that she's seen Tommy's ghost. Apparently he's been around me this whole time and I just didn't see him, but that might have changed now, right? Now that I know how to look for them, I -"

"There's no time for that right now!" he said firmly, reaching a hand up toward her. "Sally, I'm begging you, we need to move!"

"Not until I've talked to -"

"Now!" he shouted, as he suddenly saw Mildred Weaver standing directly behind her. "She's right there! You have to run!"

"You don't understand," Sally replied, still smiling. "I'm not going to go anywhere, not while Tommy's here. I'm going to find him, and I'm going to tell him how much I love him."

Behind her, Mildred Weaver slowly reached up with her hands, as if she was about to grab the back of Sally's neck.

"No!" Matt yelled, scrambling up the stairs.

"I'm going to find Tommy," Sally said, with tears in her eyes. "I'm going be with him again. Whatever it takes. And -"

Before she could get another word out, Sally felt Mildred's dead hands on the side of her head. In an instant, Mildred twisted her hands sharply, snapping Sally's neck with a sickening crunch.

Matt raced up to try to save her, but Sally's lifeless body was already falling. They met halfway up the stairs, and Matt somehow managed to catch Sally and then lower her down so that he could check for signs of life. He saw her dead eyes staring up at him, but he refused to believe that she was really gone.

"Sally!" he shouted, shaking her in a desperate attempt to get her to wake up. "Come back! Sally!"

# CHAPTER THIRTY

THE CELL DOOR SHUDDERED as a key was turned in the lock, and finally – after several hours – it was pulled open to reveal Matt's uncle Roger standing outside.

"What's going on?" Matt asked, leaping to his feet and hurrying across the cell.

"Just calm down, lad," Roger said, holding a hand up to stop him, then gesturing for him to go back over to the bed in the corner. "You and I need to have a talk."

He pulled the door shut, and then he led Matt back across the room.

"Is there any news on Sally?" Matt asked.

"I already told you about that," Roger replied, letting out a gasp as his knees clicked. He managed to sit down, and then he patted on the side of the bed for Matt to join him. "Your friend Sally Cooper died, Matt, and there's nothing to be done about that. Doctor Wilshire says it would have been quick, if that's any consolation. He's going to carry out an autopsy today and let us know the results later."

"I just thought..."

Matt's voice trailed off for a moment.

"I thought maybe there'd been a mistake," he continued finally, "or that somehow someone had managed to revive her, or that somehow she..."

His voice trailed off.

"Sit down, lad," Roger said firmly. "There are still officers down there at the pub, trying to figure out what happened tonight, and we need to get your story straight while there's still a chance."

"I didn't do anything wrong," Matt told him. "I swear."

"I know that," Roger replied, "but please... sit down."

Matt hesitated, before doing as he was told.

"I know full well," Roger continued, "that you didn't do anything to that Sally girl. You're a good boy, and you'd never hurt anyone. However, you have to admit that the situation looks bad. Your explanation of what happened to Sally isn't going to go down too well if you end up in front of a judge. They tend to take a dim view whenever people start yammering on about ghosts."

"I'm telling the truth!"

"Well, that might well be the case," Roger replied uncomfortably, "but you have to think about what's going to happen if you end up in the dock, talking about that sort of thing. There's also the fact that you weren't supposed to be in the pub at all last night, and then there's the damage that was caused, and that's before we try to link it all to the traffic accident that killed the O'Neill girl."

"Jane died because -"

"You've already told me," he said, interrupting him. "I've been around the block enough times to know that this town can throw curve balls, and that sometimes a little creative policing is required. I'm also at the grand old age where I have some influence, and I've been speaking to a few people." He paused. "You're going to be released shortly," he added finally, "and there won't be any charges. I've had a word with the folks who decide that sort of thing, so it's all going to be fine. But part of that agreement means that everything has to be kept under wraps. Do you get where I'm coming from?"

"You're not going to investigate?"

"Investigate what? A young woman tragically broke her neck after falling down the stairs. Another young woman was killed in an entirely unrelated traffic accident. Meanwhile, an old mystery about a little girl was cleared up. That's really all that people need to know, and everything'll be fine so long as you keep your mouth shut."

"You need to talk to Ernest Dwyer."

"I'm not talking to that miserable crank," Roger said, shaking his head. "Everyone knows to ignore him, he's an old fart who thinks he knows everything about this town. The day I go running to Ernest Dwyer for help is the day I know it's time to retire." He put a hand on his nephew's shoulder. "You should also steer clear of that pub from now on, because I'm not sure that you'll be Jerry Butler's favorite person right now. I hope you understand, lad, that I've stuck my neck out for you on this one and I've had to pull in quite a lot of favors. I hope you won't do anything to embarrass me."

"Of course not," Matt replied, although he was shocked that the night's events were going to end up swept under the carpet.

"I'd better go and see if they're done processing your paperwork," Roger added, wincing again as he got to his feet. "Sit tight, and someone'll be through to fetch you in a minute or two."

"Did you look at that note?" Matt asked.

Roger opened the cell door, before turning back to look at him.

"It was Dad's handwriting, wasn't it?" Matt continued. "You must have recognized it."

"My brother had the worst scrawl I've ever seen," Roger replied, "but... I have to admit, the writing on that note certainly seems familiar."

"Then -"

"And that's where we'll leave the discussion, lad," Roger added. "I meant what I said just now. You need to keep your head down and try to forget about ghosts and all that nonsense. Trust me, you'll thank me one day."

Once his uncle was gone, Matt sat alone on the bed and stared down at his hands. He kept thinking back to the moment when Mildred's ghost had snapped Sally's neck. In some small, strange way, he couldn't help thinking of the look on Sally's face. At the time, he'd assumed that she'd been oblivious to what had been about to happen, but now he found himself wondering whether maybe – just maybe – she'd understood.

And maybe she'd chosen to be with Tommy again, no matter the cost.

\*\*\*

Stopping in the hallway, Matt listened to the sound of his mother's voice coming from upstairs. He couldn't quite make out what she was saying, so he made his way quietly to the foot of the stairs and tried to listen.

"I know, Fred," she muttered with a sigh, clearly oblivious to the fact that she was being overheard, "but I worry about him. He'll be turning twenty-nine soon, and he still hasn't got a proper career."

The house fell silent for a moment.

"Maybe," she continued. "I hope you're right, but you can't blame me for being concerned. He's got no job, no girlfriend, no nothing. When's he going to get on with his life?"

\*\*\*

"Oh, it's you again," Nigel said a few hours later, as he spotted Matt making his way over to join the picket line. "Decided to finally show your face, did you? You're normally here earlier."

"I... had somewhere to be," Matt replied awkwardly, figuring that it'd be best to avoid any mention of the night's events. "What's going on here?"

"What do you think?" Nigel replied, turning and looking over at the parked police cars near the colliery's entrance. "Bloody nothing, as usual. To be honest, I'd started to think that you weren't going to show up this morning, and I wouldn't have blamed you." He paused. "You know, there are quite a few jobs on the boards in town. I even had a look myself. A young, strapping lad like you should have no problem finding something new."

"I know," Matt told him, "and I'm going to pop in later, or maybe tomorrow."

"So you've made up your mind, have you?" Nigel said. "You're going to get a new job?"

"I haven't quite decided yet," Matt told him, preferring to hedge his bets. "I suppose I'm going to keep my options open." He paused for a moment, watching the others as they waved their flags and placards, and then he looked toward the colliery's headgear in the distance. "I learned one useful thing last night, though," he added. "I learned how to see ghosts."

"Come again?"

"Never mind," he added, forcing a smile. "It's not something that'd be very easy to explain. I suppose it just means that sometimes a ghost can be right in front of you, and you don't even realize. Some people can see them easily enough, some never manage it, and some people – like me – have to learn."

"You don't half talk some rubbish," Nigel muttered.

"You don't think there are ghosts around?"

"I hope not. There are a few dead people I wouldn't want to bump into again."

Before he was able to reply, Matt spotted a figure in the distance, standing at the top of a small hill on the other side of the road. He squinted a little in an effort to see the figure better, but deep down he already knew that it was his father, even as the figure began to fade away to nothing.

"Oh, they're around alright," Matt said, with a faint smile. "Sometimes you've just got to learn to see them."

# EPILOGUE

*Three weeks later...*

"OH, TELL ME ABOUT it," Jerry said, rolling his eyes as he took the man's money and headed over to the till. "Do you think I don't hear all about that sort of thing while I'm working behind this bar?"

He took a moment to gather some change, and then he made his way back to where Bob was standing.

"I've got experts down in my cellar every bloody day," he explained as he handed the man's change over, "poking about and getting in my way, telling me that they're going to have to do some more digging just because some bones were found down there. At least the brewery's the one that's on the hook for the costs, but I'm telling you, I've just about had it up to here with experts. They get bloody everywhere!"

"It must be a bit creepy to think that there was an actual dead body in your cellar for so long."

"Not really," Jerry said with a shrug. "She never bothered me and I never bothered her, so it was a win-win situation for everyone. Now I've got half my cellar taped off just because some idiot from the local council thinks the place is a site of special historic interest. It's not a site of special historic interest, though, is it? It's a pub. It's a business. How would you like it if someone came into your car showroom and started digging half of it up?"

"It's quite interesting, though," Gary suggested.

"Is it?" Jerry replied. "Is the world experiencing a shortage of dead people? Now they're having a whip-round to try to pay for a proper funeral for the kid. Have you ever heard anything so ridiculous? The girl's dead! What does she care whether she's stuck in the ground, burned at the crematorium, or left outside somewhere to rot? Everyone's gone completely mad!"

"Jerry?"

Turning, he saw that his new barmaid Carrie was trying to pour a pint.

"The Ballylocke's off again," she told him.

"That's all I need," he muttered, turning and

heading toward the cellar door. "Don't worry, I tapped some, it'll only take me a moment to switch the lines over. I'll go, though. I wouldn't want anyone else straining themselves."

Once he was down in the basement, Jerry made his way over to the barrels and crouched down to get the new keg of Ballylocke connected. He had far less room to work in than usual, since most of the cellar was still being examined by all manner of specialists and experts, a fact that had done nothing to lighten Jerry's already rather foul mood. Even as he adjusted the various pipes, he was already muttering under his breath about all the ways that life was conspiring to annoy him.

"Where's that topper?" he said with a sigh, looking around. "Come on, I know I left it down here somewhere."

Realizing that the topper was nowhere to be seen, he got to his feet and started searching, He knew that he'd set it down nearby, which only made its sudden disappearance all the more perplexing. What he hadn't noticed, however, was that he'd managed to bump the table next to the kegs, and in the process he'd knocked the topper down onto the floor, where it now lay hidden behind a brick. As he searched with more and more anger, Jerry was also getting further and further from the spot where the topper lay.

Until, as if by magic, an unseen hand picked

the topper up and put it back on table.

"This is ridiculous," Jerry said with a sigh, before turning and looking over his shoulder, "what -"

Stopping suddenly, he saw that the topper was in its rightful place.

"I'm going mad," he continued, heading over and grabbing the topper, before attaching it to the correct keg. "Soon I'll be a drooling wreck in a bath chair."

Once everything was set up, he turned and headed back toward the stairs.

"You're welcome."

Stopping again, he realized that the voice seemed familiar. He looked back across the cellar, while telling himself that he must have misheard. Sure, the voice had sounded real, and it had reminded him a little of his recently-deceased barmaid Sally Cooper, but he knew that she was long gone. Still, the sensation troubled him for a moment, until finally he set off toward the stairs again. He briefly heard what sounded like a child, perhaps a boy, giggling, but this too he put out of his mind as he hurried up to the bar.

"All sorted," he told Carrie, as he shut and bolted the cellar door.

"So I've got a question for you," Graham said as Jerry headed back over to join his friends on the bar's other side. "It's fair to say that a lot's gone on in this pub. Not only with the girl in the wall, and poor Sally's accident, but there have been a lot of stories over the years. You've been here since, what, seventy-six? Have you, or have you not, ever seen or heard a ghost in this fine establishment?"

"Every night," Jerry replied.

"Seriously?"

"Of course not," he added, shaking his head before taking a sip of beer. "If you're going to ask daft questions, Graham, you're going to get daft answers."

"So you've not seen anything? Not even once?"

"Not even once," Jerry said, before pausing for a moment as he thought back to the voice in the cellar. He quickly reminded himself, however, that there was no point getting over-existed. Besides, the voice had probably just been caused by one of the pipes letting out a little air, and his imagination had filled in the rest. "There are no ghosts in *The Crowford Hoy*," he added, as he clinked his glass against Graham's and then took another sip. "Not that I've ever seen, anyway."

AMY CROSS

*Books in this series*

1. The Haunting of Nelson Street
2. The Revenge of the Mercy Belle
3. The Ghost of Crowford School
4. The Portrait of Sister Elsa
5. The Haunting of the Crowford Hoy

*Coming soon*

6. The Horror of the Crowford Empire

*Also by Amy Cross*

## The Haunting of Nelson Street
## (The Ghosts of Crowford book 1)

Crowford, a sleepy coastal town in the south of England, might seem like an oasis of calm and tranquility. Beneath the surface, however, dark secrets are waiting to claim fresh victims, and ghostly figures plot revenge.

Having finally decided to leave the hustle of London, Daisy and Richard Johnson buy two houses on Nelson Street, a picturesque street in the center of Crowford. One house is perfect and ready to move into, while the other is a fire-ravaged wreck that needs a lot of work. They figure they have plenty of time to work on the damaged house while Daisy recovers from a traumatic event.

Soon, they discover that the two houses share a common link to the past. Something awful once happened on Nelson Street, something that shook the town to its core.

*Also by Amy Cross*

## The Revenge of the Mercy Belle
## (The Ghosts of Crowford book 2)

The year is 1950, and a great tragedy has struck the town of Crowford. Three local men have been killed in a storm, after their fishing boat the Mercy Belle sank. A mysterious fourth man, however, was rescue. Nobody knows who he is, or what he was doing on the Mercy Belle... and the man has lost his memory.

Five years later, messages from the dead warn of impending doom for Crowford. The ghosts of the Mercy Belle's crew demand revenge, and the whole town is being punished. The fourth man still has no memory of his previous existence, but he's married now and living under the named Edward Smith. As Crowford's suffering continues, the locals begin to turn against him.

What really happened on the night the Mercy Belle sank? Did the fourth man cause the tragedy? And will Crowford survive if this man is not sent to meet his fate?

*Also by Amy Cross*

## The Devil, the Witch and the Whore
## (The Deal book 1)

*"Leave the forest alone. Whatever's out there, just let it be. Don't make it angry."*

When a horrific discovery is made at the edge of town, Sheriff James Kopperud realizes the answers he seeks might be waiting beyond in the vast forest. But everybody in the town of Deal knows that there's something out there in the forest, something that should never be disturbed. A deal was made long ago, a deal that was supposed to keep the town safe. And if he insists on investigating the murder of a local girl, James is going to have to break that deal and head out into the wilderness.

Meanwhile, James has no idea that his estranged daughter Ramsey has returned to town. Ramsey is running from something, and she thinks she can find safety in the vast tunnel system that runs beneath the forest. Before long, however, Ramsey finds herself coming face to face with creatures that hide in the shadows. One of these creatures is known as the devil, and another is known as the witch. They're both waiting for the whore to arrive, but for very different reasons. And soon Ramsey is offered a terrible deal, one that could save or destroy the entire town, and maybe even the world.

*Also by Amy Cross*

**The Soul Auction**

"I saw a woman on the beach. I watched her face a demon."

Thirty years after her mother's death, Alice Ashcroft is drawn back to the coastal English town of Curridge. Somebody in Curridge has been reviewing Alice's novels online, and in those reviews there have been tantalizing hints at a hidden truth. A truth that seems to be linked to her dead mother.

"Thirty years ago, there was a soul auction."

Once she reaches Curridge, Alice finds strange things happening all around her. Something attacks her car. A figure watches her on the beach at night. And when she tries to find the person who has been reviewing her books, she makes a horrific discovery.

What really happened to Alice's mother thirty years ago? Who was she talking to, just moments before dropping dead on the beach? What caused a huge rockfall that nearly tore a nearby cliff-face in half? And what sinister presence is lurking in the grounds of the local church?

*Also by Amy Cross*

**Darper Danver: The Complete First Series**

Five years ago, three friends went to a remote cabin in the woods and tried to contact the spirit of a long-dead soldier. They thought they could control whatever happened next. They were wrong...

Newly released from prison, Cassie Briggs returns to Fort Powell, determined to get her life back on track. Soon, however, she begins to suspect that an ancient evil still lurks in the nearby cabin. Was the mysterious Darper Danver really destroyed all those years ago, or does her spirit still linger, waiting for a chance to return?

As Cassie and her ex-boyfriend Fisher are finally forced to face the truth about what happened in the cabin, they realize that Darper isn't ready to let go of their lives just yet. Meanwhile, a vengeful woman plots revenge for her brother's murder, and a New York ghost writer arrives in town to uncover the truth. Before long, strange carvings begin to appear around town and blood starts to flow once again.

AMY CROSS

*Also by Amy Cross*

## The Ghost of Molly Holt

"Molly Holt is dead. There's nothing to fear in this house."

When three teenagers set out to explore an abandoned house in the middle of a forest, they think they've found the location where the infamous Molly Holt video was filmed.

They've found much more than that...

Tim doesn't believe in ghosts, but he has a crush on a girl who does. That's why he ends up taking her out to the house, and it's also why he lets her take his only flashlight. But as they explore the house together, Tim and Becky start to realize that something else might be lurking in the shadows.

Something that, ten years ago, suffered unimaginable pain.

Something that won't rest until a terrible wrong has been put right.

*Also by Amy Cross*

**American Coven**

He kidnapped three women and held them in his basement. He thought they couldn't fight back. He was wrong...

Snatched from the street near her home, Holly Carter is taken to a rural house and thrown down into a stone basement. She meets two other women who have also been kidnapped, and soon Holly learns about the horrific rituals that take place in the house. Eventually, she's called upstairs to take her place in the ice bath.

As her nightmare continues, however, Holly learns about a mysterious power that exists in the basement, and which the three women might be able to harness. When they finally manage to get through the metal door, however, the women have no idea that their fight for freedom is going to stretch out for more than a decade, or that it will culminate in a final, devastating demonstration of their new-found powers.

*Also by Amy Cross*

**The Ash House**

Why would anyone ever return to a haunted house?

For Diane Mercer the answer is simple. She's dying of cancer, and she wants to know once and for all whether ghosts are real.

Heading home with her young son, Diane is determined to find out whether the stories are real. After all, everyone else claimed to see and hear strange things in the house over the years. Everyone except Diane had some kind of experience in the house, or in the little ash house in the yard.

As Diane explores the house where she grew up, however, her son is exploring the yard and the forest. And while his mother might be struggling to come to terms with her own impending death, Daniel Mercer is puzzled by fleeting appearances of a strange little girl who seems drawn to the ash house, and by strange, rasping coughs that he keeps hearing at night.

*The Ash House* is a horror novel about a woman who desperately wants to know what will happen to her when she dies, and about a boy who uncovers the shocking truth about a young girl's murder.

*Also by Amy Cross*

**Haunted**

Twenty years ago, the ghost of a dead little girl drove Sheriff Michael Blaine to his death.

Now, that same ghost is coming for his daughter.

Returning to the small town where she grew up, Alex Roberts is determined to live a normal, quiet life. For the residents of Railham, however, she's an unwelcome reminder of the town's darkest hour.

Twenty years ago, nine-year-old Mo Garvey was found brutally murdered in a nearby forest. Everyone thinks that Alex's father was responsible, but if the killer was brought to justice, why is the ghost of Mo Garvey still after revenge?

And how far will the real killer go to protect his secret, when Alex starts getting closer to the truth?

*Haunted* is a horror novel about a woman who has to face her past, about a town that would rather forget, and about a little girl who refuses to let death stand in her way.

AMY CROSS

*Also by Amy Cross*

**The Curse of Wetherley House**

"If you walk through that door, Evil Mary will get you."

When she agrees to visit a supposedly haunted house with an old friend, Rosie assumes she'll encounter nothing more scary than a few creaks and bumps in the night. Even the legend of Evil Mary doesn't put her off. After all, she knows ghosts aren't real. But when Mary makes her first appearance, Rosie realizes she might already be trapped.

For more than a century, Wetherley House has been cursed. A horrific encounter on a remote road in the late 1800's has already caused a chain of misery and pain for all those who live at the house. Wetherley House was abandoned long ago, after a terrible discovery in the basement, something has remained undetected within its room. And even the local children know that Evil Mary waits in the house for anyone foolish enough to walk through the front door.

Before long, Rosie realizes that her entire life has been defined by the spirit of a woman who died in agony. Can she become the first person to escape Evil Mary, or will she fall victim to the same fate as the house's other occupants?

# AMY CROSS

*Also by Amy Cross*

**The Ghosts of Hexley Airport**

Ten years ago, more than two hundred people died in a horrific plane crash at Hexley Airport.

Today, some say their ghosts still haunt the terminal building.

When she starts her new job at the airport, working a night shift as part of the security team, Casey assumes the stories about the place can't be true. Even when she has a strange encounter in a deserted part of the departure hall, she's certain that ghosts aren't real.

Soon, however, she's forced to face the truth. Not only is there something haunting the airport's buildings and tarmac, but a sinister force is working behind the scenes to replicate the circumstances of the original accident. And as a snowstorm moves in, Hexley Airport looks set to witness yet another disaster.

AMY CROSS

*Also by Amy Cross*

**The Girl Who Never Came Back**

Twenty years ago, Charlotte Abernathy vanished while playing near her family's house. Despite a frantic search, no trace of her was found until a year later, when the little girl turned up on the doorstep with no memory of where she'd been.

Today, Charlotte has put her mysterious ordeal behind her, even though she's never learned where she was during that missing year. However, when her eight-year-old niece vanishes in similar circumstances, a fully-grown Charlotte is forced to make a fresh attempt to uncover the truth.

Originally published in 2013, the fully revised and updated version of *The Girl Who Never Came Back* tells the harrowing story of a woman who thought she could forget her past, and of a little girl caught in the tangled web of a dark family secret.

AMY CROSS

*Also by Amy Cross*

**Asylum**
**(The Asylum Trilogy book 1)**

"No-one ever leaves Lakehurst. The staff, the patients, the ghosts... Once you're here, you're stuck forever."

After shooting her little brother dead, Annie Radford is sent to Lakehurst psychiatric hospital for assessment. Hearing voices in her head, Annie is forced to undergo experimental new treatments devised by a mysterious old man who lives in the hospital's attic. It soon becomes clear that the hospital's staff, led by the vicious Nurse Winter, are hiding something horrific at Lakehurst.

As Annie struggles to survive the hospital, she learns more about Nurse Winter's own story. Once a promising young medical student, Kirsten Winter also heard voices in her head. Voices that traveled a long way to reach her. Voices that have a plan of their own. Voices that will stop at nothing to get what they want.

What kind of signals are being transmitted from the basement of the hospital? Who is the old man in the attic? Why are living human brains kept in jars? And what is the dark secret that lurks at the heart of the hospital?

AMY CROSS

## BOOKS BY AMY CROSS

1. Dark Season: The Complete First Series (2011)
2. Werewolves of Soho (Lupine Howl book 1) (2012)
3. Werewolves of the Other London (Lupine Howl book 2) (2012)
4. Ghosts: The Complete Series (2012)
5. Dark Season: The Complete Second Series (2012)
6. The Children of Black Annis (Lupine Howl book 3) (2012)
7. Destiny of the Last Wolf (Lupine Howl book 4) (2012)
8. Asylum (The Asylum Trilogy book 1) (2012)
9. Dark Season: The Complete Third Series (2013)
10. Devil's Briar (2013)
11. Broken Blue (The Broken Trilogy book 1) (2013)
12. The Night Girl (2013)
13. Days 1 to 4 (Mass Extinction Event book 1) (2013)
14. Days 5 to 8 (Mass Extinction Event book 2) (2013)
15. The Library (The Library Chronicles book 1) (2013)
16. American Coven (2013)
17. Werewolves of Sangreth (Lupine Howl book 5) (2013)
18. Broken White (The Broken Trilogy book 2) (2013)
19. Grave Girl (Grave Girl book 1) (2013)
20. Other People's Bodies (2013)
21. The Shades (2013)
22. The Vampire's Grave and Other Stories (2013)
23. Darper Danver: The Complete First Series (2013)
24. The Hollow Church (2013)
25. The Dead and the Dying (2013)
26. Days 9 to 16 (Mass Extinction Event book 3) (2013)
27. The Girl Who Never Came Back (2013)
28. Ward Z (The Ward Z Series book 1) (2013)
29. Journey to the Library (The Library Chronicles book 2) (2014)
30. The Vampires of Tor Cliff Asylum (2014)
31. The Family Man (2014)
32. The Devil's Blade (2014)
33. The Immortal Wolf (Lupine Howl book 6) (2014)
34. The Dying Streets (Detective Laura Foster book 1) (2014)
35. The Stars My Home (2014)
36. The Ghost in the Rain and Other Stories (2014)
37. Ghosts of the River Thames (The Robinson Chronicles book 1) (2014)
38. The Wolves of Cur'eath (2014)
39. Days 46 to 53 (Mass Extinction Event book 4) (2014)
40. The Man Who Saw the Face of the World (2014)

41. The Art of Dying (Detective Laura Foster book 2) (2014)
42. Raven Revivals (Grave Girl book 2) (2014)
43. Arrival on Thaxos (Dead Souls book 1) (2014)
44. Birthright (Dead Souls book 2) (2014)
45. A Man of Ghosts (Dead Souls book 3) (2014)
46. The Haunting of Hardstone Jail (2014)
47. A Very Respectable Woman (2015)
48. Better the Devil (2015)
49. The Haunting of Marshall Heights (2015)
50. Terror at Camp Everbee (The Ward Z Series book 2) (2015)
51. Guided by Evil (Dead Souls book 4) (2015)
52. Child of a Bloodied Hand (Dead Souls book 5) (2015)
53. Promises of the Dead (Dead Souls book 6) (2015)
54. Days 54 to 61 (Mass Extinction Event book 5) (2015)
55. Angels in the Machine (The Robinson Chronicles book 2) (2015)
56. The Curse of Ah-Qal's Tomb (2015)
57. Broken Red (The Broken Trilogy book 3) (2015)
58. The Farm (2015)
59. Fallen Heroes (Detective Laura Foster book 3) (2015)
60. The Haunting of Emily Stone (2015)
61. Cursed Across Time (Dead Souls book 7) (2015)
62. Destiny of the Dead (Dead Souls book 8) (2015)
63. The Death of Jennifer Kazakos (Dead Souls book 9) (2015)
64. Alice Isn't Well (Death Herself book 1) (2015)
65. Annie's Room (2015)
66. The House on Everley Street (Death Herself book 2) (2015)
67. Meds (The Asylum Trilogy book 2) (2015)
68. Take Me to Church (2015)
69. Ascension (Demon's Grail book 1) (2015)
70. The Priest Hole (Nykolas Freeman book 1) (2015)
71. Eli's Town (2015)
72. The Horror of Raven's Briar Orphanage (Dead Souls book 10) (2015)
73. The Witch of Thaxos (Dead Souls book 11) (2015)
74. The Rise of Ashalla (Dead Souls book 12) (2015)
75. Evolution (Demon's Grail book 2) (2015)
76. The Island (The Island book 1) (2015)
77. The Lighthouse (2015)
78. The Cabin (The Cabin Trilogy book 1) (2015)
79. At the Edge of the Forest (2015)
80. The Devil's Hand (2015)
81. The 13$^{th}$ Demon (Demon's Grail book 3) (2016)
82. After the Cabin (The Cabin Trilogy book 2) (2016)
83. The Border: The Complete Series (2016)
84. The Dead Ones (Death Herself book 3) (2016)

85. A House in London (2016)
86. Persona (The Island book 2) (2016)
87. Battlefield (Nykolas Freeman book 2) (2016)
88. Perfect Little Monsters and Other Stories (2016)
89. The Ghost of Shapley Hall (2016)
90. The Blood House (2016)
91. The Death of Addie Gray (2016)
92. The Girl With Crooked Fangs (2016)
93. Last Wrong Turn (2016)
94. The Body at Auercliff (2016)
95. The Printer From Hell (2016)
96. The Dog (2016)
97. The Nurse (2016)
98. The Haunting of Blackwych Grange (2016)
99. Twisted Little Things and Other Stories (2016)
100. The Horror of Devil's Root Lake (2016)
101. The Disappearance of Katie Wren (2016)
102. B&B (2016)
103. The Bride of Ashbyrn House (2016)
104. The Devil, the Witch and the Whore (The Deal Trilogy book 1) (2016)
105. The Ghosts of Lakeforth Hotel (2016)
106. The Ghost of Longthorn Manor and Other Stories (2016)
107. Laura (2017)
108. The Murder at Skellin Cottage (Jo Mason book 1) (2017)
109. The Curse of Wetherley House (2017)
110. The Ghosts of Hexley Airport (2017)
111. The Return of Rachel Stone (Jo Mason book 2) (2017)
112. Haunted (2017)
113. The Vampire of Downing Street and Other Stories (2017)
114. The Ash House (2017)
115. The Ghost of Molly Holt (2017)
116. The Camera Man (2017)
117. The Soul Auction (2017)
118. The Abyss (The Island book 3) (2017)
119. Broken Window (The House of Jack the Ripper book 1) (2017)
120. In Darkness Dwell (The House of Jack the Ripper book 2) (2017)
121. Cradle to Grave (The House of Jack the Ripper book 3) (2017)
122. The Lady Screams (The House of Jack the Ripper book 4) (2017)
123. A Beast Well Tamed (The House of Jack the Ripper book 5) (2017)
124. Doctor Charles Grazier (The House of Jack the Ripper book 6) (2017)
125. The Raven Watcher (The House of Jack the Ripper book 7) (2017)
126. The Final Act (The House of Jack the Ripper book 8) (2017)
127. Stephen (2017)
128. The Spider (2017)

129. The Mermaid's Revenge (2017)
130. The Girl Who Threw Rocks at the Devil (2018)
131. Friend From the Internet (2018)
132. Beautiful Familiar (2018)
133. One Night at a Soul Auction (2018)
134. 16 Frames of the Devil's Face (2018)
135. The Haunting of Caldgrave House (2018)
136. Like Stones on a Crow's Back (The Deal Trilogy book 2) (2018)
137. Room 9 and Other Stories (2018)
138. The Gravest Girl of All (Grave Girl book 3) (2018)
139. Return to Thaxos (Dead Souls book 13) (2018)
140. The Madness of Annie Radford (The Asylum Trilogy book 3) (2018)
141. The Haunting of Briarwych Church (Briarwych book 1) (2018)
142. I Just Want You To Be Happy (2018)
143. Day 100 (Mass Extinction Event book 6) (2018)
144. The Horror of Briarwych Church (Briarwych book 2) (2018)
145. The Ghost of Briarwych Church (Briarwych book 3) (2018)
146. Lights Out (2019)
147. Apocalypse (The Ward Z Series book 3) (2019)
148. Days 101 to 108 (Mass Extinction Event book 7) (2019)
149. The Haunting of Daniel Bayliss (2019)
150. The Purchase (2019)
151. Harper's Hotel Ghost Girl (Death Herself book 4) (2019)
152. The Haunting of Aldburn House (2019)
153. Days 109 to 116 (Mass Extinction Event book 8) (2019)
154. Bad News (2019)
155. The Wedding of Rachel Blaine (2019)
156. Dark Little Wonders and Other Stories (2019)
157. The Music Man (2019)
158. The Vampire Falls (Three Nights of the Vampire book 1) (2019)
159. The Other Ann (2019)
160. The Butcher's Husband and Other Stories (2019)
161. The Haunting of Lannister Hall (2019)
162. The Vampire Burns (Three Nights of the Vampire book 2) (2019)
163. Days 195 to 202 (Mass Extinction Event book 9) (2019)
164. Escape From Hotel Necro (2019)
165. The Vampire Rises (Three Nights of the Vampire book 3) (2019)
166. Ten Chimes to Midnight: A Collection of Ghost Stories (2019)
167. The Strangler's Daughter (2019)
168. The Beast on the Tracks (2019)
169. The Haunting of the King's Head (2019)
170. I Married a Serial Killer (2019)
171. Your Inhuman Heart (2020)
172. Days 203 to 210 (Mass Extinction Event book 10) (2020)

173. The Ghosts of David Brook (2020)
174. Days 349 to 356 (Mass Extinction Event book 11) (2020)
175. The Horror at Criven Farm (2020)
176. Mary (2020)
177. The Middlewych Experiment (Chaos Gear Annie book 1) (2020)
178. Days 357 to 364 (Mass Extinction Event book 12) (2020)
179. Day 365: The Final Day (Mass Extinction Event book 13) (2020)
180. The Haunting of Hathaway House (2020)
181. Don't Let the Devil Know Your Name (2020)
182. The Legend of Rinth (2020)
183. The Ghost of Old Coal House (2020)
184. The Root (2020)
185. I'm Not a Zombie (2020)
186. The Ghost of Annie Close (2020)
187. The Disappearance of Lonnie James (2020)
188. The Curse of the Langfords (2020)
189. The Haunting of Nelson Street (The Ghosts of Crowford 1) (2020)
190. Strange Little Horrors and Other Stories (2020)
191. The House Where She Died (2020)
192. The Revenge of the Mercy Belle (The Ghosts of Crowford 2) (2020)
193. The Ghost of Crowford School (The Ghosts of Crowford book 3) (2020)
194. The Haunting of Hardlocke House (2020)
195. The Cemetery Ghost (2020)
196. You Should Have Seen Her (2020)
197. The Portrait of Sister Elsa (The Ghosts of Crowford book 4) (2021)
198. The House on Fisher Street (2021)
199. The Haunting of the Crowford Hoy (The Ghosts of Crowford 5) (2021)

AMY CROSS

For more information, visit:

www.blackwychbooks.com

AMY CROSS

Printed in Great Britain
by Amazon